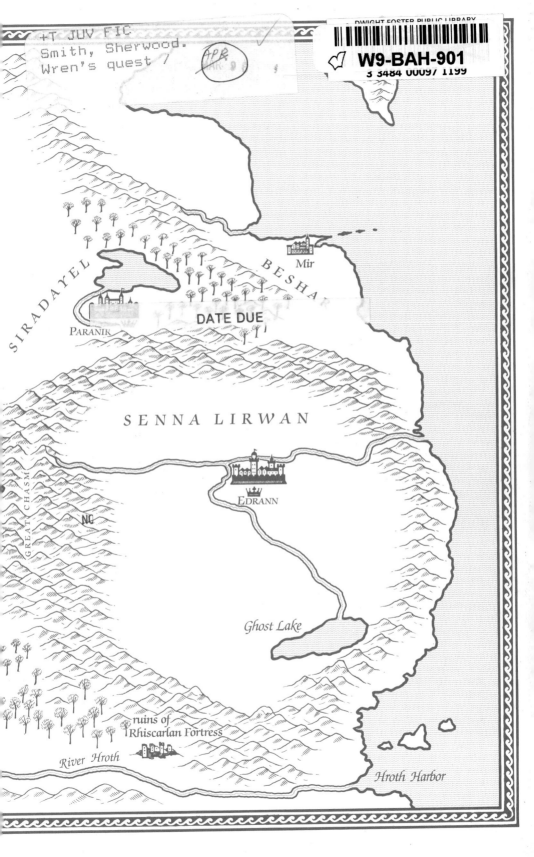

SIRADAYEL

BESHA

Mir

PARANIK

SENNA LIRWAN

GREAT CHASM

NC

EDRANN

Ghost Lake

ruins of
Rhiscarlan Fortress

River Hroth

Hroth Harbor

Wren's Quest

Also by Sherwood Smith

WREN TO THE RESCUE

Wren's Quest

Sherwood Smith

Jane Yolen Books
Harcourt Brace Jovanovich, Publishers
San Diego   New York   London

HBJ

Library of Congress Cataloging-in-Publication Data
Smith, Sherwood.
Wren's quest/Sherwood Smith.—1st ed.
p. cm.
Summary: While Wren and Prince Connor set off to uncover
her parentage, a sinister wizard creates havoc back home
in Cantimoor and threatens to kidnap Wren's best friend,
Princess Teressa. Sequel to "Wren to the Rescue."
ISBN 0-15-200976-0
[1. Fantasy.] I. Title.
PZ7.S65933Ws 1993
[Fic]—dc20 92-18988

Design by Camilla Filancia
Endpaper map by Anita Karl and Jim Kemp
Printed in the United States of America
First edition   A B C D E

To Apanage:

friends and family

Wren's Quest

ROYAL FAMILIES OF MELDRITH AND SIRADAYEL

♛ : MELDRITH

♛ : SIRADAYEL

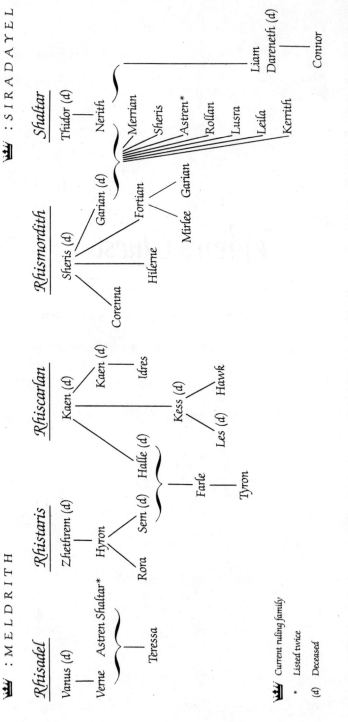

♛ Current ruling family

* Listed twice

(d) Deceased

NOTE: This family tree only shows connections relating directly to the main characters in this book. The four families are old and have intermarried many times. Anyone who wishes to know all the connections and all the cousins would do best to consult the Heraldry Guild in Cantirmoor.

Chapter One

The sound of horns playing the King's fanfare cut through the babble of conversation in the theater.

Prince Connor Shaltar stood up with everyone else, turning his face toward the royal box. The King and Queen entered the flag-draped box, and everyone bowed, including Connor. Behind the royal pair, two other figures entered: Princess Teressa and her friend Wren.

The girls were whispering, but Connor saw Wren's eager eyes taking in every detail of the theater. She saw him at the same time, and her face broke into a wide grin. Giving him a surreptitious wave, she nudged the Princess and whispered something more. Teressa looked up and smiled. It was a quiet smile—polite, Connor thought. Reserved. Quite proper for a princess to give a troublesome relative who had no land and no future.

He smiled back, then turned his eyes away so she wouldn't think he was inviting attention. As he did he remembered the relatives close by, and he braced himself for some kind of caustic comment. Scanning his relatives quickly, he realized with some relief that as soon as the royal bow had been made, the King and Queen had been forgotten.

Aunt Carlas was busy gossiping with Aunt Corenna about somebody's clothes; Uncle Fortian conversed in a low whisper with Uncle Matten while bending his cold and haughty gaze on a couple of young aristocrats in the opposite box. Cousin Mirlee was glaring at a plump, overdressed daughter of a popular baron—no doubt, thought Connor, Mirlee was counting up just how many nasty things she could say about the girl later. And Cousin Garian with his chief toady, a second cousin named Nyl, were busy staring down at the young people gathered in the first rows of the pit. A moment later Connor saw Garian slide a look around before pulling a handful of dried peas from his tunic. He handed some to Nyl, and they began pelting the audience below. Both boys were soon red-faced with smothered laughter.

That does it, Connor thought, rising silently from his chair at the back of the box. *If I tell my uncle I'll catch it hot from Garian—and if I don't, I'll catch it from my uncle. Since I'm doomed either way, I may as well get into trouble on my own account.*

He lifted aside the dusty velvet curtain at the back of the box, edged back one step, two, and suddenly he was free.

Laughing to himself, he raced down the narrow hall. But instead of taking the tiled stairs that led to the lobby for wealthy patrons, he pushed open a narrow door almost hidden in the wall carvings, and a few moments later he was backstage.

Here the noise was different; rather than the idle roar of bored aristocrats, Connor listened to the somewhat desperate gaiety of actors getting ready for a performance, a sound he knew well.

"Ho! Where's that wig, Piar?" a tall actress called, bustling by. "For my life, find that wig!"

"Pssst," came a far-off hiss. "It's here, right where it should be."

"Better you'd lost your head, that's easier to replace," an older actor cracked, and the tall actress took a swipe at him with her fan.

"Is my shirt torn? How could I have tripped over that wretched box . . ." a short, balding actor demanded, hands in the air.

Nearby, the stage magician stood, studying a new play.

2

She was young, new at her job, and Connor felt a familiar pang of regret when she waved her fingers and an illusory tree appeared. She squinted at it, then snapped her fingers, and the illusion was gone. *Supposedly the easiest kind of magic, and I can't even do that much,* Connor thought, turning away.

He wandered farther backstage. No one seemed to notice him in the increasing pandemonium, but he saw someone else looking panic-stricken, and Connor edged through the crowd toward him.

"Please, Master Salek. The last verse of my poem—I've forgotten it." That was the new player, Jeth, a fellow not much older than Connor, and as Connor drew near, Jeth threw a quick, distracted smile his way and sketched a brief bow.

Craning his neck, Connor spotted the black-gowned playwright conversing in an urgent undertone with the leading lady. Clearly he would be no help to poor Jeth, so Connor cued him obligingly: *"And lo, the price of greatness . . ."*

"is the closing of the Gate," Jeth quoted in relief. "Yes, now the rest is coming back. Thank you, thank you, Prince Connor. This is horrible—I'm already wringing wet, and I haven't even been out before the lamps yet. Those shark-toothed toffs'll take one look and laugh me off the stage." Jeth seemed to remember who Connor was then, and he flushed with embarrassment. "Begging your pardon, of course—"

"Shark-toothed they are, or at least some of them," Connor said, laughing. "Cheer up. You sounded fine yesterday, and you will again today."

Jeth continued to mutter nervously, and because he seemed to be glad to have someone to mutter to, Connor stood by and tried to be encouraging.

"Places," Master Salek said suddenly, glancing at the colored candle his assistant carried.

Connor joined the rush of movement offstage, and with a last wave at Jeth, he took his place along the wall in back.

The new prentices smoothly pulled the curtain open, the stage magician muttered softly, and illusory snow began to fall. Out beyond the gleam of the lamps along the stage's edge, a murmur swept the audience, not quite extinguishing the giggles from one side of the gallery. Connor recognized Garian's laugh, though it was abruptly cut short. Garian's father had finally caught him. They would both notice Connor's absence shortly.

He made a face at the darkness beyond the stage. Uncle Fortian would guess immediately where he was, and he would be furious. Only yesterday, when Connor had returned late from the last rehearsal, his uncle had given him the benefit of a lecture about how unseemly it was for the son of one queen and brother of another to be consorting with players. The thought of more of those lectures made Connor turn away with a sigh.

Voices from the stage caught his attention then. He cast a quick glance at Master Salek, who was whispering soundlessly to himself, mouthing the words as the actors out front spoke them. Connor felt a familiar chasm open inside him, a tremendous yearning to be sitting on that stool, wearing a black gown, murmuring his own words as voices spoke them before an audience . . .

It will never happen.

He forced the thought from his mind and gladly let his present surroundings fade from his attention. His mind sank into the magic of the play world as the familiar story unfolded.

The last notes of the horn signaling the play's end echoed into silence, and then came a roar of applause. Wren smacked her hands together until they stung. "Oh, that was wonderful," she exclaimed. "How I wish *I* could travel to another world!"

Princess Teressa nodded her agreement, blue-gray eyes shining with enthusiasm. "Will the Magic School teach you the sorcery for passing through those world-gates?"

Wren shook her head. "I wish," she said fervently. "But that kind of magic is supposed to be hardest of all. Imagine doing it wrong and being caught forever between worlds!"

Teressa shivered. "Horrible thought. Just as well I am not learning sorcery, then. I think I'd be too frightened to try."

"You've got enough scary mishmosh to learn," Wren said as they followed the King and Queen out of the royal box. The vast room of aristocrats bowing low, their satins and velvets rustling like trees in a wind, never failed to remind her that she was only an orphan of no importance. She lowered her voice and continued, "All those tables of taxes and tariffs to remember, not to mention trade laws. Foo!"

Teressa walked smoothly, smiling this way and that at the bowing people, looking as assured as if she had been doing it all her life, instead of for just a year. "I actually enjoy those things," she said. "It's like a window—you can see exactly what is coming in and going out."

Wren shook her heavy braids back. "And to think I once wanted to be a princess."

Both girls laughed. Ahead, Queen Astren turned to look at them. "We are invited to join Carlas and Fortian for supper, girls. There might be some dancing afterward."

Wren rubbed her hands together. "Dancing!" After the Queen turned back to King Verne, Wren added in a low voice, "We ought to get *some* reward if we're to be stuck staring at that sourpickle Mirlee over our food."

Teressa smiled her agreement.

They arrived at the wing of the royal palace where Teressa's uncle Duke Fortian Rhismordith lived with his family when they were in Cantirmoor. In the long, decorated dining room a magnificent feast awaited them. Good smells pervaded the crowded room: braised meats, spiced pies, and hot wine and cider.

As soon as the King and Queen entered, knots of adults broke off their conversations and gave cries of welcome. Wren saw ladies waving feathered fans with quick movements that seemed almost nervous.

With great ceremony the Duke conducted King Verne and Queen Astren to the seats of honor at a long table, leaving the girls to make their way to the table for the young people. Servants paraded in, bearing great trays of food and circulating around the adults' table.

Wren sat next to Teressa, who was at their table's place of honor. Almost immediately Mirlee Rhismordith appeared, with several followers in tow. Gowned in gold-trimmed scarlet, Mirlee looked about with her high-bridged nose elevated, her sallow face haughty. She surveyed the gathering boys and girls.

When she saw Wren she paused, making certain that Wren knew that she'd been seen. Then Mirlee deliberately transferred her gaze to Teressa. "Did you enjoy the play, cousin?" she asked in a stickily sweet voice.

"I did," Teressa answered. "And you?"

Mirlee patted her mouth, affecting a yawn. "Oh . . . it was . . . nice," she said in a bored voice. "Of course, you haven't seen many plays, have you?" The sympathy in her voice was as false as her smile.

Neatly reminding everyone within earshot that Teressa spent most of her thirteen years not as a princess should, but in the guise of an ordinary girl in a lowly orphanage, Wren thought indignantly.

Teressa's feelings did not show on her calm face. Her eyes were serious as she answered, "Not yet. But 'tis something I look forward to doing more of."

"Well, I liked the fights," Mirlee's brother, Garian, put in. "That fellow with the yellow beard knows his way around a sword."

"Yes," Nyl piped up, as usual agreeing with whatever Garian said. "Pretty knacky!"

Suddenly everyone was talking at once.

Under cover of the voices, Wren leaned toward Teressa.

"I'm glad that Mirlee thinks I'm too lowborn to notice. If she tries talking to me the way she talks to you, I'll come right back at her with some choice words about snootnoses. Not to mention just how terribly sallow skin goes with scarlet satin."

Teressa laughed softly. "She's just angry with you."

"Angry?" Wren asked in disbelief. "With me?"

Teressa smiled ruefully. "She can make all the fuss she wants about your background, but everyone in Cantirmoor knows who you are just the same."

"Oh yes. Princess rescuer." Wren buffed her nails pompously across the front of her one good dress. "Don't tell me that prissy cousin of yours wishes she'd gone into Senna Lirwan with us to get you out? If so, she could have come with my goodwill—we could have used extra help."

"Oh, it's not that," Teressa said, serious again. "She's angry because you and Connor and Tyron *did* rescue me. I think she was hoping that I'd never return and her brother would be declared the heir to the throne in my place."

Wren choked on a sip of cider. "That's—that's—I can't think of a word nasty enough," she whispered furiously.

"I figured it out a few days ago. It explains just why I'm so unpopular with her and her friends," Teressa said. "Not that I really care about them," she added.

"Who needs them?" Wren agreed. "And . . . speaking of friends, where is Connor?"

Teressa gave her head a slow shake. "He hasn't come in yet. And I know he is supposed to be here." She nodded toward an empty chair near Garian.

Wren turned to look at the rowdy boys, some of whom were shooting bread pills across the table at the girls. She especially watched Garian, who didn't look any better than his sister in bright scarlet satin. He was at the opposite end of the table, whispering with his four closest cronies. Wren recognized three of them: scrawny Nyl, always willing to do anything to gain Garian's approval, fat Perd, and curly-haired

7

Marit. The last of their group was new; Wren would have remembered that tall, sharp-faced boy with the long black hair if she'd seen him before.

"Who's that?" she whispered to Teressa. "Along with Garian's shadow pals."

"His name is Hawk," Teressa whispered back. "A nobleman's son from some foreign land."

"He's certainly picked the worst boys in court to make friends with."

"Oh, Aunt Carlas thinks they're the best," Teressa returned. "She never stops telling me how brave and smart her wonderful son, Garian, is."

Wren put her spoon down in disgust. "What? She's still trying that matchmaking poofery? And you just thirteen!"

Teressa nodded. "Awful, isn't it? I have to bite my tongue lest I tell her I'd rather marry a toad."

Wren was about to protest how awful it was to be talking about marriage at their age, but then she remembered reading in the histories that some princesses were betrothed at ages even younger than Teressa was now. Stealing a glance at her, Wren was startled to realize that Teressa's round face had started changing, showing contours that reminded her very much of Queen Astren. When Teressa gestured, pushing a lock of her long hair behind her, Wren saw that she was beginning to show a graceful figure as well. Teressa would be fourteen on her next birthday, and she was beginning to *look* fourteen.

And how old will I be? Wren thought, feeling distinctly queasy. When she'd been found, the orphanage had decided she was two, and that had been that. Supposedly, she was nearly thirteen—though she might in fact be any age. *One thing for sure, whatever age I am, I don't care at all for this talk of betrothals.*

Thinking about Teressa's future reminded Wren of her own plans. Feeling a jolt inside, she thought of what awaited her at noon the next day—the Basics Test, the most important test for a beginning magic student, and there was nothing one could do to study for it now.

She turned her attention back to Teressa and saw her scanning the room. "Connor is still not here," Teressa murmured. "And I'm afraid that Uncle Fortian has noticed."

Wren had forgotten all about the adults. Wondering how Teressa managed to keep her eye on everyone in the room, Wren sneaked a peek and saw the tall, haughty Duke at the King's right hand frowning over in their direction. "I'll wager Connor's backstage with the players," Wren whispered. "And has forgotten all about the time."

Teressa sighed. "If I go to find him, then everyone will notice."

"But I can go," Wren said, rising. "And no one will think a thing about it. I have a question or two to put to him anyway." She swallowed. "About tomorrow."

As Wren slid from her seat, Teressa gave her a smile of gratitude. Sure enough, when Wren got to the door, she saw that none of the young aristocrats were paying her the least heed.

Ignoring a look from a supercilious servant at the door, Wren walked sedately to the end of the corridor, and as soon as she was out of sight, she started running. Pausing only once, to trip the latch of an old secret passageway that Teressa had shown her recently, she dashed down the narrow stairs, then skidded around a corner, through an archway, and out into the night air. Then, putting down her head, she ran her fastest toward the other end of the palace.

Chapter Two

Wren!" Connor exclaimed. "What are you doing here?"

"Came for you," Wren said, still trying to catch her breath. Wiping a hand over her shiny forehead, she cast an admiring look around, adding, "So this is what it's like behind the stage? I've got to get back here soon."

"What's wrong?" But Connor knew as soon as the words were out. "My uncle?"

Wren nodded. "He noticed you weren't at the dinner." She pruned her mouth and looked around, her nose held high, mimicking the haughty Duke.

Connor laughed, though inside he did not feel like laughing. For a time he had escaped to the world of the play and the players—but now the real world, and all its problems, was closing around him again.

"Tess sent me."

Connor felt a cold chill. "I suppose she was angry?" he asked carefully.

Wren blinked. "Who?"

"Teressa," Connor said, even more carefully. In actuality Teressa was his niece, but he didn't feel like any kind of an uncle. He was not sure, in fact, that she really wanted an extra uncle—at least not a fifteen-year-old one who was always in trouble.

"Of course not," Wren said—*But then she would say that,* Connor thought. Wren liked all her friends to get along.

"I'll go back with you," she added. "There's going to be dancing. It will keep my mind off . . . things."

Connor made his farewells to the players, and Wren watched, her light blue eyes taking in every detail of the costumes and props. Connor remembered his own excitement the first time he'd been permitted backstage. He wondered if Wren felt the same.

They went out into the cool night air, Wren twisting around backward to take one last view of the stage area. Then she batted her wide skirts straight and said briskly, "That's another thing I'll want to look into if I—if I, well, fail."

"Fail?" Connor asked.

Wren grimaced. "Tomorrow is my Basics Test."

Connor had spent several years studying at Cantirmoor's Magic School, so he knew what she faced. "Basics already?" he exclaimed. "You *have* learned fast. Most people take a couple of years just to reach that level. Took me four years to flunk it."

Wren opened her mouth, then closed it again, giving him an uncertain look.

Connor could see her very plainly in the light of the torches on the high wall. "What were you going to ask?"

"Well," she began, "when Tyron first told me about your Basics Test last year, it seemed really funny. He said you'd, uh—"

"Turned Master Sholl into a turtle." Connor nodded. "You heard right."

"But now that I know something about magic, that seems strange. For one thing, they only ask you to do illusions and demonstrate focus and control in the Basics Test. None of us are supposed to know how to really *change* anything, much less a person. And Tyron said it wasn't just an illusion, but a real shape-change," Wren asked. "How did you manage that?"

Connor shrugged. "I don't know," he said. "No one does. That's why they finally threw me out—in the nicest

11

way possible, you understand. And I don't feel bad about it. Truth to tell, it was a relief. I was tired of being the oldest in any class and not being able to do anything right, tolerated only because of my birth. No matter how careful I was, the spells either did not work, or they went . . . sideways."

"Sideways?"

"Well, after Master Sholl tested me on rules and basic spells, he asked for illusions. I was supposed to cast one over a stone. I decided to make it look like a turtle. So I did the spell, concentrated my hardest—and the stone disappeared." Connor snapped his fingers. "And Master Sholl was crawling around on the sand, looking about as shocked as a turtle can look. Luckily Mistress Pellam had come along to observe, and she was able to restore him to his proper form. After she finished laughing," Connor added wryly. "Anyway, I don't think *I* could have restored him. And then I was too scared to try. Haven't tried anything since, in fact."

"So it really was a shape-change." Wren gave a low whistle. "I sure don't know what to make of *that*."

"Well, neither did the teachers," Connor said. "So a week later, I found myself a former student of magic. That was when I rode down to join you and Tyron on your quest to rescue Teressa from that rotter Andreus."

"Glad you did, too," Wren said, then looked around quickly. She lowered her voice. "Do you think your problems with magic are related somehow to your—talent?"

Connor shrugged, feeling uncomfortable as always when his ability to understand and communicate with birds and animals was mentioned. He, too, stole a look about, but there was no one in sight. "I don't know," he said. "Since I never told any of the teachers, I couldn't ask them. I did ask about other people having the ability, though, and no one had heard of it."

"But we don't have many people descended from the Iyon Daiyin in this part of our world; that much I've found out in my own studies," Wren said. "Those odd magical talents are supposedly more common in other lands. But you'd think a knack for *learning* magic would go along with such a magical talent."

Connor shook his head. "It doesn't. Not with me, anyway."

"Tyron says—" She stopped suddenly.

Connor never did discover what it was that Tyron had told Wren. He looked up and was startled to see a tall figure silhouetted in the yellow light spilling from the doorway. "Uncle Fortian."

Wren stayed silent, studying the Duke with an expression midway between fearful and wary.

"The Princess awaits you in the ballroom, Young Mistress," Connor's uncle said formally to Wren, ignoring Connor altogether.

"You don't know how lucky you are to be an orphan," Connor said under his breath.

Wren sketched a curtsy, then shot Connor a sympathetic look before moving past them.

"Come inside," the Duke said shortly once Wren was gone. He turned around and led the way not toward the ballroom but up to the Rhismordiths' splendid private apartments.

At least this jaw-down won't be in public, Connor thought, following his uncle's broad back up the stairs. The thought didn't help much.

"Connor!" Carlas exclaimed as soon as they entered the parlor. She clapped one hand to her head and fell back on a couch in relief. "Thank *goodness* we will *not* have to send out a search party."

Connor bit his lip. He knew that his aunt's worry was false, that she was more interested in creating a grand scene than in anything that might have happened to him, but he couldn't say so.

His uncle turned a cold look on him. "I suppose you were dallying in the theater again?" His tone made it sound worse than throwing mud on the Queen's favorite tapestry.

"Yes."

His aunt sighed, shading her eyes.

"There was always a hope," his uncle drawled, "that you had disrupted our party and worried your aunt for a *reason*. The King might have sent you on an urgent errand, or perhaps you had fallen ill and could not move. But to disappear all evening without telling anyone, after what happened to the Princess last year . . ." He lifted his hands.

Annoyed, Connor burst out, "Andreus of Senna Lirwan is not about to kidnap me!" He wished immediately that he had not spoken.

His uncle lifted one of his brows and said with even heavier sarcasm, "You've received a message of assurance from the Sorcerer-King?"

Connor fought against an angry flush that burned up his throat to the tips of his ears.

"It amazes me that you can be so certain of anything," his uncle went on, taking a turn about the room. "You did not get along with your siblings in Siradayel, so you came here. Four years studying at the Magic School, and you failed at that, too. Your mother placed you here with me so that you could learn something of the duties and responsibilities facing someone of royal birth—but you cannot seem to manage that, either. Instead, you run off at every opportunity to tarry at the heels of ragtag actors and charlatans, who probably tolerate you only because of your exalted position in society."

Connor clenched his jaw. At first, he knew, the players had allowed him in because of his "exalted" birth. But after a while he'd earned his own right to be there. Not that his uncle and aunt would look on being allowed to visit the players as any privilege, he realized. In their eyes, privilege went with money and power, not with art and craft.

"It doesn't seem to me that he has learned anything," his aunt said in a failing voice.

"I should hate to have to send you back to your mother in disgrace," Fortian added.

Connor said nothing. He realized that anything he ventured would only make things worse; his uncle was capable of turning any words against him. He just had to wait until the Duke's temper had abated, and until then try to stay out of his way.

Looking down at the beautiful carpet, he tried to study its pattern of leaves rather than listen to the biting voice list all the defects in his character. It was especially hard to have Garian held up as a good example after the business with the pea throwing at the theater—but Connor knew that Uncle Fortian could not see anything wrong with his own children.

". . . we'll try again, for the last time," the Duke said.

Connor lifted his head, hearing "the end of the lecture" in his uncle's voice. He wasn't ready for what came next.

"For your own good, I must now forbid you ever to go near the theater or the actors again. The closest you may come is sitting with us to watch the performances—and I have misgivings even about that."

Connor gasped. His uncle smiled thinly, obviously pleased with his reaction.

"You had better employ your time in the proper pursuits of a young gentleman," Fortian said smoothly. "I do not know what your mother intends for you to do with your life, but when Queen Nerith does send for you, you *will* be prepared." He made a gesture of dismissal.

Connor turned and went out, fighting against the sting in his eyes.

Wren whirled around the circle and skipped on to her last partner, breathless with laughter. She loved fast dances, especially the brannel, which allowed the dancers to add extra spins and steps.

As the dance finished, she looked across the circle at Teressa. The Princess moved with unhurried grace through the final steps, her auburn hair swinging smoothly against the back of her skirts. *How does Teressa manage to stay so neat?* Wren wondered, tucking another escaped lock of blond-and-brown-streaked hair behind her own ear.

Wren's partner turned away, chattering with another girl, and Wren crossed the disintegrating circle toward Teressa.

"My uncle is back, but Connor isn't," Teressa whispered urgently as soon as Wren was near.

"Uh-oh," Wren said. "Trouble, right?"

A faint frown creased Teressa's brow, but she did not say anything. As the girls walked toward the refreshment table Wren saw a knot of ladies look up and break off their conversation. With smiles and elegant bows to Teressa, they moved away. The Princess looked after them with a slightly troubled air.

"Why does Connor have to live with the Duke anyway?" Wren asked. "Why can't he stay with Mistress Leila? She's his sister. Duke Fortian is just an uncle."

Teressa turned back to Wren and gave her head a shake. "When Aunt Leila gave up being a princess of Siradayel in order to become a magician, supposedly she gave up her family, too. At least that's the way the rest of the family sees it."

Wren sighed, watching the tall Duke in close conversation with two other men on the other side of the ballroom. His long face wore an expression of disdain. *It would be horrible to have him as a relative—not to mention Mirlee and Garian,* she thought.

"Families . . ." she said, feeling a kind of swooping inside. She remembered her Basics Test the next day. After her test —pass or fail—she had important plans.

Teressa looked at her in concern as she sat down on a bench. "Have you really decided to try to find your family?"

Sinking down beside the Princess, Wren shook her head. "I know it's useless and impossible, and it won't matter a bit to who I am now, but still . . . every time people have birthdays, or mention their families . . . I feel something missing here." She pressed her fist against her heart. "I can't say why, but it *matters*. Everyone who says it doesn't has a family already! So I've pretty much decided that after my Basics Test, I'll use my free time to make a trip to the border castle where I was first brought and see if there's any trail to follow from there."

Teressa's eyes brightened. "I wish I could go with you."

"I wish you could, too," Wren said, giving an emphatic nod. "Well, if I fail the Basics Test I'll join a group of traveling players and seek adventure. Want to come with me?"

Teressa laughed. "After what happened last year, I think I'd just as soon hear about your adventures when you come back."

"Well," Wren said, stretching, "maybe adventure will come here and find *us*."

Wren had meant her comment as a joke, but to her surprise Teressa seemed to have taken it seriously. Almost on cue, her eyes searched the room again, and she looked—Wren thought—quite worried.

♔

Chapter Three

*T*he next morning Connor rose well before dawn. Dressing hastily, he slipped down by back routes to the practice yard at the garrison end of the palace complex. Faint light smeared the clouds in the east, and his breath frosted in the chill morning air.

Early as he was, he still saw a short, sturdy figure standing motionless in the door of the armory.

"Good morning, Mistress," Connor said softly. He hated to break the peaceful silence before he had to.

Mistress Thule disappeared for a moment, then reappeared bearing two long wooden staffs in her hands. Her face, seamed by years, weather, and experience, expanded into a broad smile. "Ready for some bruises, are ye, young one?"

"Try me," Connor answered readily. "Just try me."

The Mistress tossed him one of the staffs, and they moved into the empty courtyard. She waited while Connor swung his staff around, warming up his muscles. Connor sped up the pace of his warming moves, partly against the cold and partly to try to ease the knot of anger that seemed to have taken up permanent lodging inside him.

Mistress Thule's eyes narrowed as she watched him. As usual, she offered no comment.

Connor still didn't know why he had been singled out

for this honor—for an honor it was. Mistress Thule, as Weapons Mistress for the Palace Guard, was only slightly less awe-inspiring a figure than Captain Nad, who held the same position in the King's border-patrolling Scarlet Guard. Mistress Thule was in charge of overseeing the training sessions for the young palace aristocrats, which meant she selected the instructors and sometimes watched the practice sessions. She seldom interfered herself.

"Step out," she said suddenly, interrupting the flow of Connor's thoughts. "Start with your high defense."

Connor went through the motions with the ease of months of practice. After he'd been dismissed from the Magic School, he'd gone back to sword training with the rest of the palace boys, but he'd asked if he could continue the staff practice he'd had with the mage students.

Not that the Magic School students were taught a lot. The instruction they received was more for exercise than for the art of self-defense. Magicians were expected to get themselves out of trouble using their wits and their magic.

Connor had enjoyed the staff practice and kept up with it despite the sneers of his cousin's friends.

"Hey, watch now," the Mistress's voice cut in.

She broke past his guard and tapped his arm sharply with her staff, which made him wince. For a time he paid close attention, then his mind went back to New Year's week, when Mistress Thule had appeared at one of his practice sessions, watched without speaking, then abruptly informed Connor that from now on he'd practice with her, just before dawn, every third day. If he were late once, the lessons would stop.

Smack! She thumped him across his back. "Watch me," she commanded.

His attention turned to what he was doing and stayed there as the pace of the bout sped up.

The Mistress's staff whirled in her gnarled hands, and Connor blinked against the sting of sweat in his eyes, trying to follow the flashing wood, fend it off, maybe even break past that formidable guard. Sometimes—if he was really fast and good—she let him.

Truth was, he didn't know why he'd been singled out this way, but he liked it. In fact, if it hadn't been for the support of Tyron—and also of Wren, when he saw her—and these lessons to look forward to, his spirits would have been quite low. *Wren*, he thought suddenly. *Almost time for her Basics Test. Hope she got my poem—*

Snap! He ducked, jumped, and followed up the Mistress's retreat with a series of rapid jabs, grinning at the mental picture of Wren's expressive face and her colorful insults. What would she say when she found out about Uncle Fortian's newest decree?

He tried to force his attention back to the bout. Anger burned through him anew, lending strength to his attack and speed to the swing of his staff.

Crack! Snap! Whirling under a blurring jab, he thrust the end of his staff out and—*thwack!* The staff tapped the Mistress's shoulder.

She gave a sharp bark of laughter. "Landed a good one," she said. "Now, keep that end up. Try again."

Swiping a hand across his brow, Connor straightened up, laboring to control his breathing. His arms were beginning to feel like limp string, but he launched himself into the next bout without hesitation.

At the same time, Wren and her roommate, Fliss, sat in their room at the Magic School. Wren sighed as she gazed out at the bleak early-morning light. Fliss, a thin girl with dark, curly hair and a round, cheerful face, sighed in sympathy. Fliss knew she would be facing this very same morning next year, and she did not look very cheerful now.

"I won't make it past midmorning," Wren said. "My insides feel like they're full of rocks and my head has turned into a pumpkin. Why do they torture us like this?"

20

Fliss said practically, "If the test had been set for dawn, you would just have worried all night and wondered why it hadn't been set for the night before."

"I suppose," Wren muttered. She had slept, but not well. Nasty dreams had troubled her all through the night, making her toss and turn. She wondered if she should mention them.

They weren't just nasty, there was something scary about them. Like somebody, or something, was threatening me, she thought, remembering.

A knock sounded on the door.

Fliss jumped up to answer it. The first-year student whose week it was for running messages thrust a ribbon-tied scroll at her. "For you, Wren." He turned to leave.

"Who from?" Wren asked, reaching for the paper.

"Palace page brought it over," the boy said, then he ran off.

Opening the scroll, Wren burst out laughing. "A silly poem," she said. "About turtles."

"Who from?" Fliss asked.

"Connor."

"*Prince* Connor?" Fliss's brown eyes went wide. "Will you read it out loud?"

"No," Wren said, but she softened her refusal with a grin. Sliding the poem carefully into one of her pockets, she suddenly felt a lot better. "Let's go get some breakfast."

"Good work," Mistress Thule said at last.

That was Connor's signal that they were done for the day—and it was also high praise. When she was not pleased, she said, "You'll do better next time." Now she picked up her staff and strode briskly into the armory.

Connor followed more slowly, his staff gripped in tired fingers. He'd put it away and get something to eat, then come back down for a little sword-fighting practice. Or maybe he'd just watch—this session with the staves had been longer than any yet, and he needed a rest.

There was nothing much else to do with his time. He thought about the long day stretching ahead, then shook his head. No use thinking about the theater. He'd go over to the Magic School later, and if Wren and Tyron were free, he'd find out how Wren had done on her test. Until then—

Laughter splintered his thoughts, announcing some early arrivals to the practice yard. Garian swept in, his gaze searching this way and that. Behind Garian strolled Perd Ambur, of Mescath; Marit Limmeran, of Tamsal, on the border; and the dark-haired one Connor knew only as Hawk.

"You were right," Garian said to Hawk as they swaggered in, cloaks swirling.

What he said next Connor missed. An argument broke out between Perd and Marit about a wager. Still, those few words were enough to send a faint sense of alarm through Connor. If his cousin had been looking for him, it just meant more trouble. His cousin had heard about the theater ban, for he'd made some nasty comments the night before, and again at breakfast.

"Still favoring the clumsier forms of peasant brawl, eh, Lackland?" Garian taunted, drawing his blade and knocking Connor's staff aside. His friends laughed.

Connor swallowed an angry response and forced himself to continue on toward the door to the armory.

"Afraid to try a bout with steel?" Garian sneered.

Connor shrugged. "If you like to think so," he said.

Garian and Perd hooted. Connor ignored them.

Five steps from the armory door, Connor felt a sudden flash of pain on the back of his head. He whirled around.

Garian roared with laughter. "Good one," he crowed. "Woke him up, it did." He leaned on his blade, still whooping.

Connor rubbed the back of his scalp, feeling a warm, sticky trickle. Then he heard the ringing rasp of steel as Hawk drew his blade and tossed it hilt first to Connor.

Connor's right hand reached automatically to catch it.

"Come on, Lackland," Hawk invited sardonically. "Teach him a lesson."

Garian snorted and reached out with his blade to strike Hawk's sword from Connor's hands.

Flinging down his staff, Connor gripped the sword and moved into a defensive position. Anger made him forget for a moment how tired he was. *You've hounded me for too long,* he thought, blocking Garian's blow.

Marit and Perd promptly began calling jeers and insults, but Connor closed them out of his mind. He knew his cousin was a nervous fighter, fast with his reflexes but hating anything coming near his face. Connor feinted upward.

Clang! The swords rang together, shoulder-high. Garian blinked, backing away a step, and Connor followed up with a couple of fast moves. Tired as he was, if he was to win it must be soon.

When Garian retreated, someone laughed. Flushing, Garian launched forward with a furious attack. Again Connor feinted close to Garian's head, causing his cousin to stumble back. Then Connor reached to bind Garian's blade, hoping his grip was as slack as it looked. If he could just disengage the weapon from Garian's hand—

A sting on his arm wrenched his attention away. Perd grinned and moved in to hit Connor again, and Connor stumbled for a moment, his feet tangling with the staff.

A hot spurt of anger flared in Connor, causing him to fling away Hawk's sword and pick up the staff. Try two against one, would they? He swung the staff and knocked Perd's blade clear out of his hands.

The boy fell back, howling in pain and anger. Connor stepped aside, poking his cousin ungently in the shoulder. Swinging the staff neatly under a whistling flail of Garian's blade, he followed up with a tap on his knee.

"Here, what's this?" the voice of one of the regular instructors broke in. "Practice blades only, young sirs, you know the rule—"

Connor obediently lowered the staff, then brought it up again as Garian slashed at him.

Glaring in rage, Garian cried haughtily, "Don't interfere,

23

lackey!" To his three friends, "Back off! I can take care of him—"

But he never got to finish. Hawk, Perd, and Marit had been whispering together, and suddenly all three turned and attacked Connor at the same time.

"I hate this, I hate this, I hate this," Wren said morosely as she and Fliss walked into the dining hall. "I'd rather sit on a cactus, or be bitten by a horde of hungry fleas, or—"

A voice interrupted Fliss's muffled laughs. "Wren?"

Both girls whirled around. In relief, Wren recognized the tall, thin boy dressed in gray. "Tyron!" Wren exclaimed, making a face as the journeymage came up to them. "Come to preach dire warnings at me, or just to gloat?"

"Both," Tyron proclaimed.

He looked at Fliss, who said promptly, "I'll go get us some breakfast." She walked off, leaving Tyron and Wren alone at one of the long tables.

"Don't tell me *you've* been worrying all night?" Tyron said with a challenging grin. "Wren, who was ready to bite the wicked King Andreus of Senna Lirwan in his own fortress, afraid of a test?"

Wren grimaced, suddenly ashamed of her bad dreams. "Weren't you worried when you took yours?" she retorted.

Tyron cocked his head to one side, his bony, expressive face changing from humor to seriousness. "A little," he said. "But not about what I already knew. I was afraid they'd slip something in that I didn't know yet, and I'd stand there like an idiot. Even though the mages told me what to expect." Tyron's brows quirked. "Not that I believed what adults told me, which is why I'm here right now. It really *is* just a test of your basic knowledge. You've already proved you know it all, over and over, but the test is kind of like a practice emergency situation. You won't know exactly what to expect, and you'll have to think quickly to solve the problem they give you. But they *won't* give you anything you can't handle."

24

"I feel like I've forgotten everything," Wren said.

Muttering softly, Tyron gestured, and a little green wart-nosed monster lumbered across the tabletop, its inch-long teeth snapping at Wren's hand.

Wren's fingers wove swiftly in the air, she pointed, and the illusion disappeared with a faint *pop!*

"*Sure* you've forgotten," Tyron said, getting up. "Look, Master Falstan is waiting for you. Eat a good breakfast, and then go out there and show him. You might even have a good time."

Connor laughed, his staff humming as he swung it. At first the four spread out, trying to come at him from all sides, but Connor's rapid smacks on head or shoulder or leg forced them back. Gestured together by Hawk, they whispered.

"Here, I'll have to report your names to the Mistress," the instructor said, coming toward them.

Distracted by the instructor, Connor almost missed it when the four suddenly charged him in a group. There was a flurry of steel and wood and arms and legs, made suddenly worse when the instructor waded in, trying to separate them. Connor stumbled back, driven by a sword-hilt blow to his stomach.

Perd also backed away, cursing loudly and holding his arm. But Marit gasped, and Connor looked down at the ground, stunned by what he saw.

His cousin lay stretched out unconscious, a cut on his scalp bleeding freely onto the dusty ground.

"Look what you did." Marit pointed accusingly.

"But I didn't," Connor began, "I—" He stopped. The yard was suddenly full of people, but none were listening to him.

"Come along inside. The Mistress will want to talk to you," the instructor said, taking the staff from Connor's unresisting fingers. "You gentlemen as well," he added, pointing to Perd and Marit. He looked around, but Hawk was nowhere to be seen, and the instructor gave a shrug and turned his attention to Garian. "Help me get this one inside," he added to another instructor, who moved quickly to help lift Garian.

Connor followed, his mind completely blank.

"Shall we get started?" Master Falstan said to Wren.

Wren nodded, trying to still her pounding heart. She reminded herself of what Tyron had said as she followed the senior mage to the Magic Designation place. Transfer magic took them to a peaceful, secluded grove that Wren did not recognize. She had no idea how far from Cantirmoor she was—but she liked the flowering fruit trees and the tall ash surrounding her. She liked what she saw, except—

That sense of warning prickled along the back of her neck, just as in her dreams. She set her bag of magic books and tools down, looking around more carefully.

"You won't need your scry-stone or your spell book," Master Falstan said, pointing at her bag.

Wren forced herself to smile. "I know—Tyron told me. But I just like to take these them everywhere I go."

She shook her head, telling herself she was being a cowardly dunce. *It's like waiting for a thunderstorm to strike,* she thought, finding the feeling difficult to shake.

Giving Wren an encouraging smile, Master Falstan scratched his thick beard and waited for her to indicate she was ready.

She smiled back gratefully. He was one of her favorite instructors, and she had been glad when she found out that he was to test her. Though some of the students thought his slow lectures were boring, with their many references to events in history, she had always found them interesting. He was also unfailingly patient and kind.

He wants me to do well, she realized. Squaring her shoulders, she pronounced, "I'm ready."

"Name the Crisis Rules," he said.

"One: A calm and clear mind hears what must be heard and provides a course of action when . . ." Wren spoke without faltering, steadied by the old familiar rules she'd learned her first week.

"The Twelve Natural Laws," Master Falstan said next.

"The world is finite, and finite, too, are the magic and material resources. Number Two: Magic that makes changes in living and nonliving things is called True Magic. Three . . ."

When she finished she took a deep breath.

"Sight-illusions, first a stationary one, then a moving one," Master Falstan said.

Wren felt a warning pang in her temple and shook her head again. Master Falstan frowned a little, and Wren, afraid he thought she was faltering, hastened to cast a spell making a tall crystal archway appear. A cold wind worried at her braids as she dispelled her archway, and she shivered, then concentrated on the spell for a moving illusion. She waved, and a purple rabbit appeared. Wren's eyes narrowed as she focused on making the fantastical creature move.

"Good," Master Falstan said, dispelling it effortlessly. "Now, your turn to dispell what I give you."

His hands wove rapidly, his lips moving in his beard. Creatures and strange objects appeared one by one, all leaping, dancing, and slithering about. Wren worked as rapidly as she could, trying to dispell each illusion as soon as it appeared.

The fretful breeze tugged at her clothes, making the backs of her arms chill. Master Falstan paused in his illusion casting and looked around in mild bewilderment, as if his concentration had been broken, then suddenly his eyes went wide.

"Wren—" He gasped and fell to the ground.

Overhead, a black cloud had formed, and now it started lowering toward them menacingly. As Wren gave it a frightened look, a branch of blue-white lightning flashed out and stabbed the ground between her and the motionless sorcerer.

Chapter Four

*Y*ou think *this* is fun, Tyron?" Wren muttered, looking up fearfully at the lowering cloud. What to do?

She could feel another lightning charge building up. Unlike a real thundercloud, this gray mass had a distinct feeling, a *focused* feeling. She realized suddenly that the lightning was going to strike again, soon, *right here.*

Fear and panic nearly overwhelmed her, then she recalled the words she'd just spoken about keeping a calm mind. She forced everything out of her head except the problem at hand.

Protection spell.

Plunging her hand into her bag, she yanked out her book. With trembling fingers she flipped the pages, seeking a recent lesson. She found the spell and spoke the words clearly, imagining a protective bubble curving overhead, covering her and the fallen magician. She *saw* it—and relief mingled with a deep sense of accomplishment flooded her when she finished and the spell held.

The cloud still hung above them, but the sense of threat had disappeared. Just as she looked up, the lightning struck again, this time directly overhead. It crackled over her bubble and splashed a spectacular spray of liquid light on either side, driving into the ground. Wisps of smoke rose from the burned grass.

All right, my bubble'll hold for now, she thought, diving for her bag. *But if THIS is an easy test, Tyron and I are going to have a few choice words very soon. For now, let's just see who the joker with the lightning is.*

She knew it wasn't Master Falstan, because he still lay motionless on the ground. Forcibly she cleared her mind again and pulled out the brand-new scry-stone she had recently been given. With careful fingers she held the crystal up. Looking into it, she sought the magician whose magic still lingered outside her bubble.

What she saw was a fanged mask, which momentarily surprised her. *Mages who don't want to be scryed can make illusory faces,* she thought, recalling another new lesson. *But a good magician can look past the masks . . .*

Wren knew she was good at scrying. She gritted her teeth, *seeing* past the mask to . . . to . . .

The other magician halted in the middle of a spell, the mask not hiding startlement. For an instant she caught a glimpse of a blurred face, then the magician vanished from the stone-vision. At the same moment the cloud overhead dissipated into swirling scraps of dark fog that disintegrated rapidly, leaving nothing but the trees, grass, still air—and Master Falstan's form lying nearby. Since the magic connecting her to the unknown magician was gone, Wren knew that her scry-stone was now useless.

Bending over the fallen magician, Wren examined him worriedly. His face was white, his breathing slow and difficult. Alarm spread through her.

"Master Falstan? Sir?" she said, taking hold of his shoulder and shaking gently.

He did not stir.

All right, then, she thought, looking down at her palms. They were sweaty. She wiped them slowly down her tunic, her thoughts speeding. She and Master Falstan were alone here, as far as she knew—unless that other magician was located somewhere nearby. She did not want to find out.

She reached for her bag again, then hesitated. Her instinct was to use magic to get them back to the school, but she had been forbidden to try transportation magic until she reached the next level. She already knew the spell, and she had even done it once—luckily for her, nothing bad had happened. But that was before she had known just how dangerous this kind of magic was.

Still, she could not see any other way out, so she crouched down with her bag in her lap, and with one hand she took a firm hold of Master Falstan's arm. With her other she carefully made the signs, a vision of the school's Designation Room fixed in her mind.

The magic swept over them suddenly. . . . There was a moment or two of grayness, and they transferred.

Wren gasped with relief, then shut her eyes. Vertigo whirled her vision. She had never transported another person before.

Their appearance set off an alarm inside the school, and almost immediately two senior magicians ran in, looking concerned.

"I hope I passed," Wren said, her voice croaking like a frog. Sitting abruptly down on the worn carpet, she put her head between her knees.

"Never again," Tyron said to Wren some time later. "I will *never* tell another student not to worry about the Basics Test." He raised a hand solemnly. "From now on, I will do my best to frighten them out of their skins."

They sat together in a small room at the school, waiting for Master Halfrid to return. As soon as Wren had related what had befallen her, the King's Magician had gone directly to the secluded grove to try some kind of magic search while the other magicians looked to the removal of the spell from Master Falstan.

And though Tyron was supposed to be teaching classes, he had stayed with Wren ever since. Feeling tired and dispirited, Wren began to wonder if they really believed her after all. "I suppose I'll get blamed for doing magic I'm not supposed to know yet."

"What?" Tyron asked, blinking.

Wren clamped her jaw shut. Just thinking she might be faulted for breaking those rules made her feel sick inside.

Tyron's face changed from laughter to shock to horror, a variety of expressions on his foxlike face that any other time would have drawn at least a grin from her. Tyron was not one for hiding his feelings.

"You can't be serious!" he exclaimed.

"Well, here you are, not that I don't appreciate it, but you've missed at least two classes, just to watch over me like—like—" She gave up and shrugged.

"That's in case whoever pulled that business on Falstan decides to come back and finish the job," Tyron said. "Mistress Ferriam is staying with Falstan for the same reason, until they find out who that mysterious magician was. Meanwhile I'm here to *protect* you."

Wren sighed. "So that's why they were all so grim. At first I thought I was going to faint. Then I just thought I was going to lose my breakfast. And meanwhile they just kept asking me questions, some of them over and over again. Then I got dumped here. With you."

Tyron thrust a hand through his unruly brown hair, making it stand up in all directions. "They don't know what to think or how to act—nothing like this has ever happened to anyone on a Basics Test. At least within living memory. Except Connor's situation, but that was different," he added hastily.

Something in his changeable face alerted Wren, though, and she said in alarm, "They're not accusing *Connor?* They couldn't—" She stopped when she saw the dismay in his brown eyes. "But they *can't.* Why?" she demanded.

"Imagine how I feel," Tyron said. "He's my best friend!"

"But that doesn't make any sense," Wren cried. "Connor doesn't know any magic—or rather, it doesn't work for him. And even if it did, he wouldn't hurt anyone. Ever! He even sent me a poem to cheer me up—"

Tyron hunched over, worry evident in every line of his

bony form. "It doesn't make sense to me either," he said. "But apparently they have a reason. I understand he's been in some trouble with his family lately, and they seem to think . . ." He shrugged, unable or unwilling to finish his thought.

"Trouble made by others," Wren said. "I've heard from Tess about the kind of trouble that skunk of a Garian causes."

Tyron shook his head. "So maybe he's getting back at everyone—"

"You *don't* believe that?" Wren demanded.

"Of course I don't," Tyron retorted with some heat. "That's what *they* are saying. So I have to sit here with you instead of helping them investigate, because they know I'll defend him. Just like he defended me when we were both beginner students."

"I didn't know that," Wren said. "What happened?"

"Haven't you heard stories about Renic the Rotten?"

Wren smiled at the name. "I thought he was made up to scare us."

"Oh, he was real, all right." Tyron made a nasty face. "He was around during my first year at the school."

"What happened?" Wren asked.

Tyron shrugged. "Well, there I was, a scrawny nine-year-old who loved to show off how much he knew. Connor was new, too, but he was popular, and he made friends easily. He could have stood aside when Renic started picking on me—a lot of other students did. They were all afraid of Renic, and some of them didn't like me because I was younger but had already started moving ahead faster. Some of them were even too afraid to tell the teachers about Renic's rotten tricks—like me." He laughed. "I loved magic learning so much that my fear of somehow being blamed for my problems with Renic was greater than my fear of the boy himself. So I didn't tell the teachers, either."

"Why did he hate you so much? Just because you were ahead?"

"I was already learning illusions and I'd figured out some

other things, but I wouldn't teach him any tricks ahead of his group. Connor saw this going on and stood up to Renic. He even camped outside my room a few nights. And when it became obvious that Renic was getting worse, not better, it was Connor who went and told Halfrid."

"The teachers hadn't *noticed?*"

"Well, they had to some degree, but since he always attacked me when they weren't around, they didn't know how bad it was. I think they wanted to give him lots of time—in case he changed for the better. But Renic was awfully sneaky, and he lied a lot. So they threw him out. Last I heard he was prenticed at a stone quarry. I hope a boulder falls on his head," Tyron added. "Might improve his outlook."

"I wondered about that," Wren said slowly. "Everywhere I've ever been, you find all kinds of people. That usually means a plentiful supply of bullies and blowhards among the good ones. But—so far—not here."

Tyron gave her a twisted smile. "Well, that's no accident. None of the seniors want to be responsible for training somebody who'll turn out to be a wicked sorcerer. That's why you beginners spend all that time memorizing the laws and rules and discussing them endlessly, before you learn one real spell. The senior magicians learn more about you than you do about the laws and rules—though you're not supposed to know that yet."

"So you think I passed Basics?"

Tyron laughed. "You kidding? You handled that as well as any of us would have—maybe better."

"I'm just sorry Connor couldn't learn magic," Wren said. "Even worse, though he just jokes about it, I get the feeling he feels bad as well."

Tyron nodded soberly, staring off far beyond the wall. "I know." Then he sighed. "Well, I guess we—"

He stopped when the door opened and a short, balding man entered, his silvery hair and beard floating about his head.

"Master Halfrid!" Wren exclaimed in alarm.

The King's Magician's customary expression was one of merry goodwill. Now, however, he looked serious.

"Wren, do you recognize this handwriting?" He held out a sheet of folded paper, on which half of three lines of writing could be seen.

Wren couldn't make sense of the words, but the tall, slanting letters and the flourishing capitals were instantly familiar.

"Easy," she said. "That's Connor—uh, Prince Connor's handwriting."

"You're certain?" Master Halfrid asked.

"Well, I received a poem this morning in handwriting just like it, and it was signed by Connor," she said.

"Poem?" Master Halfrid's brows went up. "May I see it?"

"As it happens, I carried it with me. For a boost." Wren pulled the letter from her tunic pocket and handed it over. "What's wrong?"

The Master smiled a little as he read it, but when he handed it back he was serious again. "Maybe you should take a look at that."

Wren unfolded the paper she'd been handed. On it was written:

It's about time you fools learned what real sorcery can do. Unfortunately you and your precious school won't survive the experience.

Wren's mind went numb.

When she looked up from the note, Master Halfrid went on, "I found that on my desk just after you and Master Falstan disappeared. This was right after Prince Connor was taken into custody for having apparently attacked and knocked out his cousin."

Wren dropped the paper to the floor. "I just don't believe it!" she exclaimed.

34

Halfrid held up a finger. "Wait," he said. "No judgments yet. Just observation. Tyron? Do you recognize it?"

Tyron bent and picked up the paper, then he asked for the copy of the poem. After a time he glanced up, looking confused. "Something's wrong," he said. "But I'm not sure what. Maybe it's just that I'm too upset to think—"

"Exactly." The Master smiled benignly. "Don't we waste hours of breath telling you that a calm and clear mind is *most* needed when things are at their worst?" He leaned forward and touched the scrap of paper containing the threat. "Feel that," he said.

Tyron carefully felt the paper, frowning. Then his brown eyes widened suddenly. He held the paper out to Wren, who took it and rubbed her fingers over it.

"Not like that—*feel*," Tyron said.

She shut her eyes and reached with her inner sense—and there was the faint glow of magic. Very distinct when she touched the paper, it disappeared when she lifted her hand away.

She opened her eyes. "What does that mean? Are we sensing leftover magic from when the letter was sent, Master Halfrid?"

"Wrong," Tyron said, giving his head a shake. "That kind of spell would disintegrate almost immediately. This has that feel to it because the magic is still in force. In other words, somebody got hold of Connor's handwriting and used it as a model to magic this note. Have you ever seen writing that even?"

Wren looked at the poem again and compared the two papers. She nodded, excitement growing as she saw the irregularities, the differing pen widths in the poem. "And he tried to write his best, you can see that. But this thing—not even Mistress Leila can write *that* neatly." She looked up in surprise. "So somebody put this together to make sure Connor got the blame."

"Correct," Halfrid said.

Tyron looked grim. "I'm going to find out who, you can count on that."

Halfrid raised a hand. "Gently, gently," he said. "Remember, as yet our unknown magician does not know we are aware this letter is false. Shall we keep this to ourselves for a time?"

Wren said nothing, but Tyron agreed. "What have you in mind?"

"For now, just this. You are nearly due for your weekly visit to the palace, are you not?"

Tyron groaned. "Standing around at formal court, learning etiquette! That's the last thing I want to be doing when there's—"

"There's investigating to be done, and it's being done," the Master interrupted calmly, his usual good humor back and gleaming in his eyes. "As for your visit to court, this is a sublime opportunity for you to observe who might be interested in discussing the events of today."

"Right," Tyron said, snapping his fingers. At the thought of something definite to do, his face shone with excitement. "I'd better go change into my good tunic."

He vanished through the door.

Master Halfrid smiled at Wren. "I'm glad to say that Falstan is fine," he said.

"What happened to him?" Wren asked. "Why did he fall down like that?"

"It was a sleep spell. He was too busy making spells for you, Wren, to realize something was amiss until he'd been put out. You did well, which was the first thing he said when he woke, I'll have you know."

He nodded in approval, and Wren gave a sigh of relief.

"We'll have to postpone the next students' tests until we get all this sorted out, I fear," Halfrid went on. "Now to you."

Wren felt a flare of alarm, until she saw the smile on the Master Magician's face.

"Mistress Leila told me that you intend to use the free time you've earned in a personal quest."

Wren nodded. "I want to find out where I came from—if I can," she said, reaching into her bag. She pulled out a worn sheet of paper, saying, "Just after New Year's I wrote to the orphanage where I was first brought, and someone copied out what was in their record book and sent it to me." She handed Halfrid the paper.

He squinted at the difficult handwriting.

"It's pretty much what they told me all along," Wren said. "Which isn't much. Nothing was found with me, and I couldn't talk. They named me Wren, and that was that."

Master Halfrid tapped the paper. "According to this, if you wish to find out more, you must visit the Siradi Border Guards and look at the records written by the patrol who found you."

"And that's what I want to do," Wren said. "Unless you're about to tell me I can't," she added, looking at him doubtfully.

Master Halfrid shook his head. "You have earned your first break, and I don't intend to interfere in your private pursuits, child. But I do have a request to make."

"What can I do?" Wren asked eagerly.

Master Halfrid smiled at her in approval. "Here's my idea . . ."

Chapter Five

Connor glanced at the tray of congealing food and dropped his fork. Getting up from his chair, he walked to the window and gazed out over the King's Park, where treetops stirred in the wind.

He'd been confined to his room in the palace since morning, and as yet no one had come to speak to him. He would stay because he'd promised to stay—but not knowing what was being said against him disturbed him more as the day grew longer. Several times he'd resisted the temptation to dash out and try to find someone to listen to his side.

Finally he turned away from the window. He knew he should eat, but he was too upset to be hungry. Sitting down wearily, he was just reaching for the bread when he heard a light tapping on his door.

"Come in," he said.

The door opened, admitting two of his half-sisters.

First was Astren, Queen of Meldreth, who had left Siradayel to marry Meldreth's King the year Connor was born. Connor rose promptly, executing a polite bow. Tall and beautifully gowned, as befitted a queen, Astren greeted Connor in her soft, musical voice. Her eyes were kind but searching.

Behind her came Leila, who had renounced being a Princess of Siradayel in order to become a magician. Short and red-haired and straight-backed, in the plain white robes of the magicians, Leila strode in briskly and stood on tiptoe to kiss Connor's cheek.

"I didn't hit Garian, that I'll swear—" Connor began. He did not expect to be believed.

So he was considerably astonished when Leila lifted a hand to interrupt him. "We know that," she said. "Mistress Thule saw the end of your scuffle from the window upstairs. She did not see who struck Garian, except that it wasn't you."

"This was told to us in private," Astren put in, adding, "*After* a lot of other people came by to attest to your character, and Garian's friends all came in to demand justice."

"So what's going to happen?" Connor said.

"Well, our dear Uncle Fortian has seen fit to demand a hearing at Formal Court." Leila put her nose in the air.

"Verne has granted it, of course," the Queen said, "but you and Garian will not be present. We seem to have too much taking of sides over a small issue as it is . . ." She paused, and the two adults exchanged looks.

Leila wasn't that many years older than Connor, but her manner sometimes made her seem part of their mother's generation. She said in a crisp voice, "We can't tell you everything, but the fact is, your problem is not the only one being aired everywhere. It is as if some kind of ill-natured wind has swept through Cantirmoor of late. Squabbles and feuds are becoming the common way, and as friends take sides they form factions. Some people are using your problem with Garian as an excuse to make trouble about some . . . other matters."

Again they exchanged looks.

Connor hated being left out, but if he really wanted to know what problems they were having, he had a secret way of finding out—by talking to animals. His real interest now, however, was in solving his own problems.

"So Uncle Fortian wants a formal hearing," he said. "What does that mean?"

Astren frowned a little. "He wants to force Verne to send you back to Queen Nerith."

39

Connor noticed that Astren did not call her *Mother*. He wondered if all of his siblings felt as isolated from their imposing parent as he did.

"So what Verne is going to do is listen to Fortian, and to the yard instructor who Mistress Thule sent over to give his account. Then he's going to confine Garian to the palace for two weeks for disobeying the instructor's order, and he's going to confine *you* for a month, but he's not going to say where," Lila said.

"Everyone will assume you'll be at our retreat at the lake," Astren added smiling. "A pleasant place, but watched over by the Scarlet Guard, so no one can get in—or out—without our knowledge."

Connor swallowed. It seemed so unfair, but he thought he could understand the reasons. And he knew he could find plenty to do at the lake.

"And you *can* go there, if you like," Leila said. "But actually, and the reason we're here right now when we both should be other places, is that we have another idea."

"You'd better tell him," Astren murmured. "I suspect I'm already late—court is supposed to be gathering for supper right now."

"Go ahead," Leila said. "We'll settle this on our own."

Again Connor bowed, and the Queen went out, closing the door.

"Let me tell you what else happened this morning," Leila said. "You know that Wren was to do her Basics Test."

"Yes. I'm sure she passed; Tyron says she's really good."

"Oh, she passed all right, though she and Master Falstan nearly got killed in the process."

"What?" Connor exclaimed. "How—"

"An attack by an unknown magician." Leila went on to give a brief account of what had happened, then added, "No one outside the school knows about this yet—except for Verne and Astren, of course."

Connor nodded. "I won't talk of it to anyone, but I still

don't see what this has to do with my . . ." He felt a sudden chill. "Unless—unless the target of that unknown magician's spells wasn't Master Falstan, but *Wren*."

Leila's eyes glinted. "You are quick, little brother. It struck me as interesting that two of the people who rescued Princess Teressa from Andreus of Senna Lirwan last year have suddenly gotten themselves into difficulties."

"And Andreus is known for his long memory," Connor said. "But wouldn't you magicians know if he were nosing around? And nobody has done *magic* against me." He shrugged, looking down at the untouched food.

"Yet you still seem to find yourself in trouble a lot," Leila said. "Some of it, such as your interest in plays and Uncle Fortian's disapproval, can be explained. But today's fight . . . You didn't start it, did you?"

"No. They came into the yard, and I got the feeling Garian had been looking for me, that he really wanted a fight." Connor looked up, startled. "But you can't be thinking that *he* is somehow allied with Andreus?"

"We don't know what to think—yet," Leila said. "And we can't be sure that all these troubles aren't just coincidence, of course. Which is why Astren and I had this idea. Wren wants to go up to the border of Siradayel on a private quest. By Halfrid's command, as far as anyone outside the school knows, she's traveling to Rainbow Lake to look for buried magic artifacts from the days of Tre Resdir. The idea is to see if anyone tries to follow her."

"So where do I come in?"

"As escort," Leila said. "Halfrid and I both think Wren is pretty good at taking care of herself, but it wouldn't hurt to have someone along just in case."

Connor fingered a cold piece of bread. "Has anyone spoken to Wren about this?"

"Yes, Halfrid did. She said she'd love to have some company on an otherwise boring walk, and she knows about the incident with Garian. Well?"

Relieved, Connor said, "A chance for freedom over prison? Of course I'll go. And I promise I'll do my best to help her."

"I know you will," Leila said. "The thing is, if you two are to get out of Cantirmoor without anyone knowing, it must be done at once. Tomorrow Verne is going to send a carriage to the lake with an illusionary Connor inside, guarded by a very real detachment of Scarlet Guards. Then Halfrid is going to have Tyron drop hints about Wren's trip to Rainbow Lake at his next court visit, to see who seems most interested in the details. By then you two should be well on your way. Hopefully, by the time you return, we'll have solved our various problems here."

Connor dropped the bread onto his plate. "Then I'd better pack," he said.

"I *do* hope this rain lifts, or we're going to have a soggy start," Wren said a few hours later, turning away from a window high up in the palace.

"You're going to be slogging through muck whether it stops or not," Tyron said, saluting her with his cup of hot chocolate. "*Squish, squish, squish*—mud between your toes —soggy sandals—it'll be *good* for you. Make you tough."

"Sure wish *you* were going." Wren made a face at him.

Tyron laughed, then said, "I wish I could go, too." He looked over at Connor and Teressa, who both sat straight on their chairs, silently sipping their cocoa.

Wren rolled her eyes. She'd been so glad when she'd been invited to have dinner at the palace. A last chance to see Tess and to have some laughs! And when she'd found out that the boys had been invited, too, she'd looked forward to a great evening.

Unfortunately, Teressa had withdrawn behind her polite manners, and as for Connor, he just sat there, equally polite and equally stiff. *Does he not want to come? Is he being forced to go with me?* She repressed a groan.

42

Tyron cleared his throat. "Have you picked your route?"

"I studied the school map," Wren said. And after another short silence, "It will be great fun to travel again. As long as we don't meet any villains."

Teressa set her cup down. "I wish I could go with you," she said in a low voice. "I hate the thought of staying behind to worry."

"But if Andreus is going to try something, you'll probably be his first target, not Wren," Tyron said. "You don't want to repeat your visit to his charming castle in Edrann, do you?"

Teressa smiled a little. "*That* treat I'll skip, thank you. But I would so love to be free to travel—" She slid a glance at Connor, then stopped, and shook her head. "I'm being silly," she finished. "I'm sorry. Never mind."

Wren sighed, plumping down onto the cushion next to the Princess. "It's *not* silly to want to travel, Tess. We talked about it so much when we were in the orphanage."

"But to complain as if I don't enjoy my duties here . . ." Teressa looked down at her hands.

"Saying you'd like to travel isn't complaining—" Wren started.

But Teressa's face stayed averted, and all Wren could see of her expression was seriousness. Whatever Teressa felt was not going to be changed by arguing.

"So I'll scout things out on this trip," Wren said. "Maybe you can go next time." She spoke in a heartening tone, and she was rewarded when Teressa glanced up and smiled.

"And I'll look forward to hearing about it when you get back," Teressa said.

As if I were a stranger, and not her best friend, Wren thought. Once again, Teressa had withdrawn behind that formidable shield of good manners.

Tyron gave a sharp shrug with his bony shoulders. Wren could see that he was also bothered by the strained atmosphere. "Taking your scry-stone?" he asked.

"Got it here." Wren patted the knapsack next to her stool. "Mistress Feriam gave me some extra coaching just

43

before I came over. I'm only to use it in an emergency—but at least I know how to do *that*."

"Good. Keep up your practice with the minor spells, too," Tyron said.

Wren nodded. "I plan to."

She looked around—more silence. Sighing again, she reached for the silver pot and poured another cup of hot chocolate. It was going to be a long evening.

Wren was still thinking about the party when she set out with Connor just before dawn.

The rain had lifted, and the weak light in the east shone gray through the ragged clouds. Puddles reflected the sky here and there, but she knew that the roads would be good and flat for a long distance yet, thanks to King Verne.

A warm meal was inside her, and she felt ready for adventure. If only Teressa had been able to say what was bothering her.

And what about Connor? What was bothering *him*?

Wren slid a doubtful look at the figure marching along next to her. Dressed in plain clothing—a sturdy dark green tunic and a dull gray cloak, twin to hers, with a water-resistance spell on it—Connor carried a long walking staff in his hands. In those clothes he didn't look like a prince—and he didn't seem to mind. Wren scanned his face as he watched a flock of starlings wheeling over the grassy fields.

Wren and Connor had passed beyond the northern edge of Cantirmoor just before sunup, escorted along seldom-traveled paths by two of King Verne's close-mouthed personal guards. Coached by Tyron, Wren had been ready to cast an illusion around them if necessary, but no one had stopped them, no one had seen them. Wren was relieved—this new spell was difficult, and she hated the way the magic distorted one's vision.

Just a little while ago the guards had turned back. Since then not a word had passed between Connor and Wren.

Wren broke the silence first. "Do you feel funny about being smuggled out of the city like that?"

Connor blinked, as though his thoughts had been far away. He smiled. "You don't mean funny-*ha*, but funny-strange?"

"That's it." Wren nodded. "Tyron told me last night, after you and Teressa were gone, that as magicians, we might have to get used to tricks and stratagems. Still, I feel kind of like a thief without her sack of stolen goods. I mean, it would be different if we were sneaking away from some villains, but from our own people?"

"We have villains among our own people," Connor reminded her. "Or we wouldn't have to sneak. Anyway, I'm just glad I'm not being exiled to the lake for something that was not my fault."

So why the bad mood? she thought. And because she liked things to be clear, she asked, "Did they *make* you come with me?"

Connor looked over in surprise. "Not at all."

Wren sighed. "It's just that last night—" She stopped, suddenly remembering his problems with his family, and flushed. Fishing for a quick subject change, she said, "Do you know a good walking game?"

Connor looked thoughtful. "No—walking trips are new for me. But I do know . . . something . . ."

"Well?" Wren prompted.

"It's not a game," he said slowly. "It's a play. About Tre Resdir and the Wizard Morayen discovering Rainbow Lake. I could read it—"

"Oh," Wren said, trying to show some enthusiasm. "I know that play."

Connor laughed. "It's not that old one in the yellow-bound book, with all those stiff-sounding verses that were popular two hundred years ago. It's a new play. Still interested?"

"Yes!" Wren exclaimed. "I love the stories about Tre Resdir almost as much as the ones about Eryn Beyond-Stars.

Did the Queen allow you to take a book from the palace?"

"Not exactly," Connor replied. "You might say it is copied out."

"Will you read some now?" Wren asked.

Connor unslung his pack. Pulling a sheaf of papers out, he began reading, at first in a quick, self-conscious voice. They walked on, to the rhythm of the play. But as the story progressed, Connor began changing his voice to fit the different roles. When Wren laughed at the funny parts, he acted some of it out, waving his scroll about until Wren was afraid it would fly off across the fields.

They were both thoroughly engrossed in the story when Connor's reading began to falter, as if he'd misread words. He stopped once or twice, frowning over the text, until Wren said, "What happened? Did you get so excited you started copying the words wrong?"

Connor grimaced. "It looks that way, doesn't it? I shall have to be more careful." He smiled then, his eyes questioning. "So you like that play so far?"

"Yes, indeed!" Wren exclaimed. "No one has said, 'Hark ye! Do I bespy me a challenge?' like they all did in that play in the yellow book. Not to mention all those long, dreary speeches during which nothing happened."

"Supposedly those speeches were making fun of the politics of the time, and the audiences loved them," Connor said.

"That's what Tess said," Wren admitted. "But I don't find politics funny *any* time. I like this play: the characters talk like real people, and a lot is happening. Why don't you save the rest for later?" she suggested. "Don't want to use it up too soon."

"A good idea."

"Mind if I practice some magic?" she asked. "Just some illusions, to keep up my speed."

"I'd enjoy it."

For a time they walked along in silence, Wren decorating the unexciting countryside with bright-colored illusionary creatures. Making the illusions move was harder, for she had

46

to animate them with her mind. That meant *seeing* them move, then *directing* them to move the same way. She knew that some magicians could do this effortlessly, but she couldn't. Especially while walking. So she practiced.

After a time she said, "I've been thinking . . ." And the red-and-blue-striped snakes she had been animating broke apart in a shower of sparks.

"About?"

"Those stage magicians who make the snow and monsters for the stage plays. It might be fun to prentice out to them, if I don't make it past journeymage. How much do you know about getting that kind of work?"

Connor shook his head. "Nothing, really."

"Would you ask next time you're with the players?"

Connor looked pained. "It might be a long time," he said. "My uncle has forbidden me to visit them while I still live with him."

"Oh," Wren said, and she coughed.

The silence that had become so companionable now stretched embarrassingly between them. To distract them both, Wren made some illusionary purple toads hop out from under a shrub. Connor laughed at their goggle eyes and warty faces. Wren sent them hopping across the road, then made them vanish with a snap of her fingers. "Think we should stop and eat?"

Connor scanned the far horizon. "I think we'd be better off if we ate while walking," he said.

"Uh-oh. More rain." Wren squinted westward.

"Well, we do have this," Connor said, reaching into a pocket in his tunic. Wren heard the promising jingle of coins. "My sister gave it to me this morning."

Sister. Wren felt a pang of envy. *I'm not going to muff this quest*, she thought with determination. *By the time I'm walking back along this road, I will know who MY family is.*

"So we can stay at an inn, if we reach Wendle-on-Reth by sundown. We can also hire some horses without occasioning any questions," Connor went on.

47

"I guess two horses missing from the palace stable would have been a trifle suspicious," Wren said. "Though I didn't think anyone would notice two gone from so many."

"The stable hands know every one of those mounts," Connor said. "And they gossip a lot."

"As much as the toffs do?"

Connor laughed. "Nobody gossips as much as my esteemed and highborn relations," he said.

That put Wren in mind of something. Stealing a sidewise look at Connor, she asked, "Uh, you *do* know what it is we're looking for, don't you?"

"No," Connor said with a smile. "Leila told me to ask you about that. Whatever it is, of course I'll help—but right now I'm just glad to be getting away from my pit of hissing relatives."

Wren remembered his bitter statement two nights before: *You don't know how lucky you are to be an orphan.* She hesitated, then said cautiously, "You don't number Tess among those snakes, do you?"

"No," he said. "I don't. Nor Astren nor Leila. Nor Verne."

She rubbed her jaw. It was time to tell him about her quest. If Connor was going to think her a total fool, better to get it out in the open now.

"We're going to Pelsir Castle," she said. "Where the western part of your Siradayel border patrol keep their records."

"Something having to do with your studies?"

"Something having to do with me," she said, her eyes on the horizon. "I'm going to look up everything they have written down about that caravan where I was discovered, and I'm going to find out where I come from."

Connor was silent for a time. Birds twittered high above, and a cold breeze startled ruffling the long grasses around them. "I do believe we should pick up our pace," he said presently. "That rain will be here sooner than we'd expected, long before we reach an inn."

Chapter Six

Though they walked quickly, the storm was quicker. It overtook them late in the afternoon, and it and the roads, which were no longer smooth and well kept, slowed them down.

The wind ripped at them fiercely, sending icy rain and hail down their necks. Afraid Wren's small body would be blown away in the gale, Connor fixed his hand on her shoulder. She did not protest—or at least if she did, the howling of the storm made it impossible to hear.

Shading his eyes, Connor squinted down the road, wincing against the sting of the hailstones. He thought he saw a faint but steady yellow gleam. The town—at last? He couldn't be sure they were even on the road anymore. Darkness hid their surroundings, and the ground ran with water.

They stumbled on, guided by a flash of blue-white lightning, until Connor saw a jumble of buildings under storm-lashed trees. Then they both began to run clumsily against the wind.

When they reached the lee of the first building, the sudden cessation of the wind almost made them drop into the mud. Wren gasped in relief, leaning against the ivy-covered wall.

"The inn should be just a few steps farther." Connor pointed.

Wren shoved away from the wall, uttering a long and expressive groan that made Connor laugh.

Bracing themselves, they rounded the corner. The storm tore at them with renewed power, and Wren lost her balance, sprawling in the mud. Connor sprang after, hauling her up. Neither spoke as they staggered on.

Connor was able to spot the inn only because it was on the main road. In the increasing storm, the light from the many windows was invisible until they were right next to it. The inn's sign creaked and banged, and when a sudden flicker of lightning illuminated it, he saw a bright orange crown painted over an acorn.

"We found it!" Connor shouted.

Wren flung herself at the door, and they both fell inside.

At once figures leapt to their aid, one of them fighting the door shut again. Connor stood panting in the warm, spice-scented air. Next to him Wren shivered violently, trying with stiff fingers to drag off her gray cloak.

"Here, young ones," a cheerful female voice said behind them. "I'll help. Bad day to be traveling, eh?"

"There's room in the stable, and it's warm and dry enough," a deep male voice said firmly. "Unless you have coin."

Insulted by the idea of being dismissed to the stable, Connor frowned and touched the pouch at his side. The inn-keeper, a huge, jowly man, nodded, and his stern look gave way to curiosity and a smile.

The woman who had spoken to them was tall and stout and gray-haired, and she had never stopped smiling. She helped Wren get her cloak off, then took Connor's as well, bearing the dripping garments off toward the back. The inn-keeper said, "Follow me."

He led the way upstairs to a small room that, Connor discovered, they were expected to share with two other trav-elers. About to raise his voice in protest, he saw Wren look about, then nod. "This is quite nice," she said. "I suppose we're to have the hammocks—both those beds have some-one's gear on them."

"No beds left," the innkeeper said. "Except in the big room we save for the Duke's folk when they come through here. Screen's in that corner there. You can change behind that, and we'll have some supper waiting down below. Comes with the price, which is two lil each."

Glad Wren had spoken before he could lodge his protest, Connor dug the lily-stamped silver coins out of his pouch and handed them over while Wren exclaimed, "Great! I could eat a sea monster." As soon as the innkeeper left, she added, "Who goes first? I just hope these waterproof knapsacks really are waterproof, or I'll be exchanging one soggy tunic for another."

"You go ahead." Connor gestured, sinking down onto a bed. His feet ached in his wet boots.

Wren gave a wry laugh. "I hope you never have to wear a real disguise," she said as she rummaged in her pack.

"What?" Connor guessed at her meaning, and felt heat flood up his neck into his cheeks.

Wren nodded. "You were looking around like something smells. *Just* like a toff. If you want their big room, I guess you're entitled if anyone is. But then maybe someone might remember us." She looked doubtful.

"It's all right," Connor assured her. "I shared a room when I was a magic student. I just momentarily forgot old habits."

Wren disappeared behind the screen. "Just don't turn up your nose at the food—unless it's really terrible," she called out.

"No chance of that," Connor promised. "I could eat *three* sea monsters."

Their second set of clothes having come through the storm relatively dry, they were both soon comfortably dressed. Finding their way down to the big common room, they squeezed onto a bench at an already crowded table. A moment later a freckle-faced girl about their own age appeared, set three tankards down with a thud in front of other patrons, and turned to Connor and Wren. "Ale or cider?"

"Cider," Wren said, and Connor nodded.

The girl disappeared in the throng, and Wren sat back, looking around with an air of appreciation. She didn't seem at all bothered by the crowded table, the noise of nearby patrons carrying on jovial conversations at the tops of their voices, or the group singing ballads in the far corner. Catching Connor's gaze, she leaned forward.

"This is only the second time I've been in one of these places," she confided. "It's so big! Are the toff inns as big as this?"

"Well—they're different," Connor said, with a quick glance around. Wren obviously did not feel any sense of lurking danger. Did his own bad feeling come from a real threat, or merely from being so tired? No one in the room looked the least bit villainous.

Wren looked thoughtful. "Magic students're supposed to work their way when they travel, and use coins only in an emergency. See, I was given five lils. At this rate, they'll be gone by day after tomorrow."

"Keep your money," Connor said. "We'll use it if we run through mine."

Wren shrugged. "I won't really care about sleeping in a stable, if it comes to that. I like the smell of fresh hay, and I love horses."

The girl reappeared, carrying two big mugs in one hand and four plates balanced on the other. She clunked the mugs down in front of Wren and Connor, dealt out two plates, and swung away with the other two.

Connor examined his share: a thick stew with a pile of boiled greens alongside it. A big carved wooden spoon lay with its bowl in the food.

Wren examined her mug critically. "The ones I made

when the orphanage tried to prentice me out to the pottery in Three Groves were about like this. I wonder if they buy a local prentice's work." Without waiting for an answer, she picked up her spoon and dug in.

Connor tasted his food more cautiously. It was hot and savory. He plied the spoon with more enthusiasm.

Wren finished first, then sat back with a happy sigh. "I do like travel."

Connor returned a polite answer and kept his attention on his dinner. He still felt uneasy about nearly betraying his aristocratic origins, and he sent another covert glance around the inn room. No one evinced the faintest interest in a pair of hungry prentice-aged travelers.

Next to him, Wren sent increasingly long gazes at the growing number of people sitting around the fireplace singing and laughing. Finally she dropped her spoon onto her empty plate and stood on the bench, peering over the tops of people's heads.

"It's a minstrel," she exclaimed in delight. "A real traveling minstrel. I think the thing he's strumming is a tiranthe, but I couldn't really see it—and we certainly can't hear it over the noise. I want to get closer."

Connor watched her dash across the room. She paused for a moment, bouncing on tiptoe to see over the heads of the crowd, then she dodged between the adults and disappeared. The serving girl pushed her way through just then, and the crowd parted. Connor got a glimpse of a spindle-shanked man dressed in faded, grimy minstrel blue, strumming on a long wooden instrument. The tiranthe's shimmery, metallic-sounding chords reached Connor just as he saw Wren squeeze her way into the front of the crowd, her mouth open to join in singing the chorus.

Still uneasy, Connor did another scan of the room and again saw no danger. He finished his dinner more slowly. When he was done, he sat back and listened to the folk songs, a few of which he recognized from his days as a magic student.

The music began to change, and presently Wren reappeared. "They're starting on the love stuff now," she said, wrinkling her nose. "They'll not stop *that* all night. Whoosh, I'm sleepy, and my feet feel like a pair of bricks—except bricks wouldn't ache, would they? I couldn't shut my eyes last night, and that on top of fighting that storm makes me feel like we've been on the road two weeks, not one day."

"Agreed," Connor said, glad to be getting out of public view at last. "Why don't we essay those hammocks?"

Their room was far enough from the noise to be quiet. The thick glass in the window even diminished the steady hiss of the rain, rendering the sound almost comforting. The room was warm, and as Connor climbed into his hammock, he heard the soft thud of paws, and a moment later a plump inn cat leapt up and settled, purring loudly, on his middle. The sound of the rain, the warmth, and most of all the cat's purr made the sense of danger he'd felt all evening ease.

It must have been just tiredness, he thought, letting out his breath in a sigh and slipping effortlessly into sleep. When their roommates came in, he roused briefly at their whispering, then he dropped back into his dreams and did not awaken until morning.

The innkeepers' son was the server at breakfast. As he set down big plates of steaming food, he said, "I'm to tell anyone going north that there's been word of brigands robbing travelers in Northwood."

Wren thanked him. The server moved off, and Connor said, "I wonder if my uncle knows about these outlaws."

"Why should he?" Wren asked. "Oh. Rhismordith land, is it?"

"His barons should be protecting the towns—and fixing these roads, for that matter. Instead they are all in Cantirmoor making trouble in order to get control over the lands down south that used to belong to the Rhiscarlans."

"Is *that* what all the political noise has been about?" Wren said in disgust.

"I think so." With a quick glance around, Connor added, "Though maybe we should talk about it later."

"We don't have to talk about it at all," Wren said, spooning generous dollops of honey onto her stack of fried oatcakes. "Boring! Except, if the parents of those friends of Garian's are anything like their sons—"

"Worse," Connor put in.

"—then they shouldn't be in charge of a pigpen, not that the King will ask *my* opinion. So let's talk about something else."

"Let's eat up and get on the road," Connor suggested. "If we get over the bridge before noon, we should be able to reach Riverfall before sunset."

The inn staff had dried Wren's and Connor's wet clothes, which they packed up again. Connor paid extra for a travelers' meal—sliced bread stuffed with cheese, meat, and greens. Assured that they would find streams along their way, they did not have to fill water bags at the well. Connor asked about hiring horses, but the inn had none to spare.

They set out on foot under a scoured blue sky. A brisk wind played with their hair and clothes. As they strode along, Wren sang some of the songs she'd heard the night before, and she cast illusions to punctuate the verses. Connor watched her fanciful animals cavort across the road and disappear, and as always he felt an intense longing inside.

He'd wanted so badly to learn magic. The feel of it in the air when the senior magicians performed great spells—how to define that sense? Colors shone deeper, light stronger, and the air seemed to glimmer with *promise*. At those times he'd been so sure all he needed to do was raise his hands and make . . .

And nothing. Or—once—disaster. Not even the simplest spell worked for me, he reminded himself.

He knew he was lucky in his ability to communicate with animals and birds. Maybe that somehow equaled the magic that even the slowest student at the school eventually learned.

His attention turned to the road when he heard the

sounds of mounted travelers overtaking them. Snapping her illusions gone, Wren looked curiously back at the newcomers.

The sense of danger that had been quiescent since last night awoke in Connor once again, and his hand tightened on his staff. A moment later, though, relief washed through him as a party of merchants trotted by, followed by several guarded wagons.

Connor and Wren stepped off the road in order to allow the cavalcade to pass, then resumed walking. A short time later they rounded a hill and found themselves at the crest of a shallow river valley.

"There's the bridge!" Wren cried, pointing.

Way down in the valley, the River Reth curved northward, wide and slow and silver in the sunlight. Over its great width a bridge stretched, a monument to the efforts of artisans and magicians.

"It's beautiful," Wren enthused. At Connor's nod, she went on, "Do you remember that lesson?"

"How the bridge was built?" Connor asked. "Master Falstan went on about it at great length. It was one of the first lessons we learned."

"You found it boring?" Wren looked surprised.

Connor shrugged. "I take it you didn't."

"Nothing at the school is boring," she said. "I liked that lesson because it showed me that magic doesn't *make* things, it . . . alters things. Or moves them. Or joins them with other things. I really didn't understand it until they told us about the bridge, step by step."

Connor nodded, too polite to disagree. He'd found the careful explanation about the building of the bridge mildly interesting—but mostly he'd fought against disappointment. The magic in it didn't seem to be real magic. He'd never been able to express that feeling properly, since he *knew* it worked. Perhaps that was the first lesson that made him aware that magic would be forever inaccessible to him . . .

So what was the magic he sensed in the air around them? This kind was different than the kind the magicians had taught the students: stronger, and so vast. In the past, when he traveled high in mountains, or when the weather changed very suddenly, he could almost see it, like light on diamonds . . . *Forget it,* he told himself. *Haven't you had enough failures?*

Two roads converged, and Wren and Connor suddenly found themselves walking in a long line of travelers. Wren smiled as she looked about.

"There isn't much chance of brigands dropping on us now," she said. "Isn't it lucky that the storm kept so many from traveling yesterday?"

Connor fought once more against that curling sense of danger, and he forced himself to smile back at her. "Yes, it is," he said, reaching into his pack. "This looks like it'll be slow going, getting over the bridge. Shall we eat our lunch on the way?"

Steady walking brought them into Riverfall, a small town tucked up against some hills opposite a spectacular cataract. Wren admired the fine green lawns stretched between well-kept houses with patterned tile roofs. At first she was delighted with the town, but her enthusiasm faded a little when it became apparent that all the other travelers on the road had decided to stop in the same place, and there were no rooms to be had at any of the public inns.

"Here's my thought," Wren said finally, putting her hands on her hips. "The night is nice enough for us to sleep outdoors, if we can find a good grassy spot."

"After we eat a hot dinner." Connor jingled the coins in his bag. "We'll stay warmer with hot food in us."

"I'm for that." Wren rubbed her hands. "Let's go back to that place where I smelled the fruit pies baking."

They had to wait for a place to sit down, but before too long they had a snug corner of a table not too far from the fireplace. Their tablemates were all around their age, and most of them were friends—a group of weaver's journeymen and prentices being sent to a trade fair. Wren saw Connor withdrawing behind his mask of politeness, so to draw attention away from him, she talked volubly, asking questions and answering theirs with made-up stories about being a potter's prentice.

As she talked, Wren slid a few indirect looks at Connor. He was frowning, just as he had the evening before. *What was wrong?* She'd have to ask him as soon as they were alone.

The food came at last, hot and good and plentiful. For a time their table was quiet as everyone dug in. The girl to Wren's right looked up once to ask for the salt cellar, and Connor reached to get it—then he paused, his hand midway across the table as he stared at the door on the far side of the room.

Startled, Wren turned to see what had caught his attention. Expecting anything from armed soldiers of King Andreus to a monster, she was relieved that it was only a pair of young men wearing the blue tunics of Duke Fortian's family.

Connor quickly pushed the salt into the hands of the waiting prentice, then he turned in his seat so that the young men scanning the room saw only the back of his head. Wren decided to hide as well. Scrunching down in her seat, she raised her mug to her lips and drank. The mug effectively blocked her face from view.

The young men scanned the room, then they turned and left.

"Connor? Aren't those—"

"Later."

When they went outside at last, Wren and Connor both checked the roadside. People were strolling about in the balmy air, most of them heading across the green toward the moonlit falls.

"Wren, can you use that stone of yours to find out if

anyone is scrying us?" Connor asked. "There may be some trouble . . . some danger. I've had this feeling . . ."

Wren was silent a moment, considering. "I can use the stone if I have to," she said at last. "Why? Weren't those two messengers from your family? Those were the Rhismordith colors they had on."

"Yes, one of them is Marit Limmeran's stepbrother."

"Well, we don't know they are searching for *us*," she said. "Even supposing they are, how do you know it's trouble? Maybe they need to give you a message."

Connor shook his head. "Think, Wren," he said. "Think. My sisters went to a lot of effort to make it look as if I were being taken to the King's house on the lake, down south. If Astren needed to contact me, she'd send one of the King's messengers. And if Leila wanted me, she'd contact you by magic somehow. *My Rhismordith relatives shouldn't know I'm here.*"

Wren's back suddenly felt cold.

"If they were Lirwani spies, chasing us for some nefarious purpose cooked up by King Andreus, I'd know what to expect. But these are in somewise cousins. Supposedly allies."

Wren stared at him. "What you're saying is, we might have an enemy after us, but it's not somebody from outside the country—it's someone from Meldrith?"

"I've got to figure out why," he said in a low voice. "There must be a *reason* why nearly everyone in my family is suddenly my enemy. There must be a *reason* why I feel danger all about us. I don't think it is only my imagination. Can you use your scry-stone?"

"I can try," Wren said, "but it would help if you knew what we sought. Also, you should know that I'm not supposed to be using the stone for real scrying. Practice, yes. But—"

"But you *could* tell if someone were trying to find us, couldn't you?"

"Yes. Well, maybe." She took a deep breath, searching

for the right words. "It's not quite like looking out of your eyes for someone in the physical world. At least, not for me. I don't know enough yet. If I start looking through the stone, then my presence is there to find for anyone who is already looking, and I don't know how to close out unwanted listeners, or hear only one, or any of those complicated things. So the other person is going to know just where I am and will even be able to spell me from a distance, unless I'm really careful and really fast."

"They'd get our location?"

"Easily."

Connor looked away for a moment. "Wren—" He turned back. "I don't wish to interfere with your studies, and I know that sometimes wizards keep certain things secret. But you don't have any other quest, do you? Besides this search for your forebears, I mean?"

"That's it." Wren spread her hands. "I swear."

"But somebody didn't want you to pass your Basics Test," he said. "And if the Rhismordith Blues *are* looking for me, then somebody went to a lot of trouble to find out that I'm not at the lake. *Why?*"

Chapter Seven

"All right," Wren said. "It's time to be practical. We don't really know it's us being looked for, but you've got a feeling about it."

She saw Connor nod, his silhouette dark against the moon-touched falls.

"You think it would be a bad idea to go up and ask those messengers."

"I do."

"And it could be your uncle who sent them, but it could also be Garian? Garian can command those fellows to go do things?"

"He can."

"The thing that doesn't make sense to me is how that business with Master Falstan and my Basics, and you and your trouble with Garian, might connect," Wren said. "Unless Garian has thrown in with Andreus of Senna Lirwan and is willing to help him get back at us for rescuing Teressa. Could *that* be why Garian's pestering you?"

"Maybe," Connor replied. "Except nothing has happened to Tyron, and he was also with us on the rescue. Garian hates the sight of me and has let everyone know it, but I can't see him taking orders from anyone, especially a hated enemy like Andreus. He was furious when he wasn't permitted to go with the army last year when everyone thought it would come to battle. I just don't see him joining Andreus's side."

61

Wren sucked on her lower lip, thinking rapidly. "Perhaps. But I think he's really a follower. Oh, he might be the first to call insults, but that kind rarely thinks of things. He just takes over someone else's ideas as if they were his own. So maybe someone is leading him on?"

Connor had wrapped himself in his cloak, and Wren couldn't see his face, but she could tell by the angle of his head that he didn't believe this. "Perhaps. But in all my encounters with Garian, he led his gang, never they him."

"All right, then," Wren said. "Let's try another idea. When I was in the orphanage, the bullies often went after someone who had something they wanted."

"Impossible," Connor said. An echo of his earlier intensity colored his voice when he added, "I have absolutely nothing. No land, no inheritance—and not even the prospect of a job."

"I thought you wanted to be a stage player? Oh yes. Now your uncle won't even let you visit them."

Connor mumbled something inarticulate.

Wren went on, "Sorry, Connor. So it's not that. Huh! Garian is the Duke's heir, right? So he'll have plenty someday, never mind how unlucky those poor people are to be stuck with such a terrible lord. Maybe by then Teressa will be Queen, and she can make him behave and tend to his lands. That doesn't help us now. All I can say is, let's keep clear of your Rhismordith Blues and be glad they aren't nasty Lirendi spies, and for now that's that." She stretched out her cramped legs. "Oh—about that inheritance business."

"Yes?"

"Well, I know you don't get anything for being Queen Nerith's eighth child. But how about your father? Wasn't he a duke?"

"Yes, but when he married Queen Nerith he gave his sister, my aunt Yura, his lands in order to prevent political problems, and he carried the title only as long as he lived." Connor laughed a little. "You can imagine how welcome I am among my Dereneth cousins, all of them thinking I'm going to try to get those lands back somehow."

"Phew," Wren said, shifting about so she could lie flat on the grass and stare up at the gleaming stars. "Glad I don't have to deal with that. I don't think I could ever keep it straight who gets what, when, and why."

Connor laughed again, and silence fell.

Wren sighed, thinking, *At least we lowborn types don't have that kind of trouble. You pick a job, and you do it . . .* But even as she thought it, she remembered some of the gossip among the weavers at dinner. They'd been fluent and bitter about their master's son, who was apparently a terrible weaver and had a worse personality. But his father, blind to all that, had made it clear that this son would inherit the family business. *I guess it's not that simple for anyone. Except an orphan.*

She thought about being responsible only for herself. That seemed so neat and tidy somehow. If she was good at her work, she'd do well. And if she turned out to be a poor magician, she'd no doubt go hungry. No family to push her ahead—or hold her back.

Yes, that's how it should be, each responsible for herself. Or himself. Still, here I am, trying to find my family.

For the first time she wondered if what she was doing was right. Connor had the best kind of family—certainly the highest in worldly rank. Yet they weren't doing him a bit of good.

But as soon as she considered the idea of giving up her search and going back to Cantirmoor, she got the old lost feeling again. *If I do find my family and they turn out to be monsters, at least I'll know,* she thought. *Then I can forget them and go right back to making myself what I want to be.*

As she started to slide into sleep, she thought about a visit she'd made to Fliss's home when Fliss and her cousins had giggled in the attic, sharing family jokes. *Belonging,* Wren thought sleepily. *That's what I want.*

She turned over and slept.

63

Sunlight crested the rocks above the falls and shone in Wren's eyes. She sat up, delighted to find that they had picked a beautiful sweep of parkland to sleep in. A natural wall of shrubs surrounded them on three sides, and on the fourth a cliff jutted over the river below. The muted thunder of the falls was underscored by the trilling of a line of birds flying high in the sky.

Wren saw Connor's head tip back, his eyes intent on the flock.

When the birds had passed by, she said, "What're they talking about?"

Connor shrugged, looking slightly uncomfortable. "They don't—talk, not like we do."

"So their song meant nothing?"

"That's not right either. I wish I could explain . . ." He paused, concentrating, then said, "It was mostly about food. Food and nesting."

"Mmmm." Wren rose to her feet and stretched. "What good is it to be able to eavesdrop on birds if they never say anything interesting?"

Connor smiled as he stowed his cloak in his knapsack. "What do you expect from birds?" He bent and picked up his staff, swinging it back and forth, round and round.

"Bird-wits." Wren hastily fixed her long braids, then beat the grass off her cloak before putting it away. "Going to be warm today."

"Shall we get an early start?"

"*After* a good breakfast," Wren said. "Good, hot, and lots, if you get my drift."

Connor grinned. "Do you hear me arguing?" Still, he looked around carefully as they crossed the green toward the public inn. And when they reached the door of the common room, he paused and scanned the room before going inside.

No one disturbed them, though; they ate well, bought some extra food to carry with them, and then set out on their walk. Again, no mounts were available for rent, and while they could have bought horses with Connor's bag of money, they both felt that to do so would attract undue attention.

The weather was fine. Almost every traveler going to the north seemed to have chosen the winding river road instead of the shorter one through the great Northwood Forest. Apparently the word about brigands had gotten around.

Wren was glad to see other travelers on the road, but Connor scanned everyone who overtook them, on the alert for any more of his uncle's equerries. Any time they heard someone approaching from behind, Connor insisted they step off the road until he could see who was coming. If the far-off figures wore blue, Connor and Wren waited in the shrubbery until the travelers went by.

"If we're going to be sitting in these bug-infested bushes a lot," Wren said finally, batting at a flying insect near her face, "let's make it worthwhile. How about if you read more of that play? We were just getting to the place where Tre Resdir meets Morayen."

Connor had been squinting down the road at the approaching travelers. "I see blue," he said. "Shhh."

Wren sighed, sitting back on her heels. At least the thick shrubs kept them from being splattered with mud, she reflected as the cavalcade passed by.

"Ordinary folk," Connor reported, rising. "Good."

"Again," Wren said, adding sourly, "I wonder if everyone in Meldrith is wearing blue these days."

Connor gave her an apologetic smile.

"So can we have more of the play?" Wren asked as they started walking again.

"Well . . . there isn't much more," Connor said slowly.

"You mean you only copied out a portion of it?" Wren could not keep the disappointment from her voice. "What good is that? That's like inviting someone to dinner and leaving them in another room to smell the food."

Connor laughed, his face reddening.

Watching, Wren made an astonishing discovery. "Unless," she said slowly, "you weren't really copying it. You're *writing* it. You're making your *own* play!" She yelled the last.

Connor winced, his face now crimson. "Shh-hhh."

"Why? There's no one coming—thank goodness," she added, eyeing the thornbushes they were passing. "Your own play! How? Why? Does anyone else know? So that's what you meant when you said you wouldn't be a player, and I got the feeling you meant something else. Argh," she added, clapping her hands to her ears, "I'm full of so many questions my head feels like a beehive."

Connor shook his head, smiling. "I love those plays so much, I thought I'd try to write one," he said, looking down at the ground. "I think I could happily spend my life watching my words spoken onstage."

"Can you do that?" Wren exclaimed. "Oh, of course you can," she said doubtfully.

Connor gave his head a quick shake. "If I do finish this, I'll turn it in at the Playwrights' Guild with a false name on it. I don't want to be treated as Prince Connor; I want to know if I'm really good enough to try to prentice out to the playwrights."

"This is exciting," Wren exclaimed, rubbing her hands. "But you haven't told anyone? Not even Tyron?"

Connor looked away across the fields. "Tyron is a great friend," he said, then paused.

Thinking about Tyron, Wren said, "He hates plays, I remember that from our journey last year. Well, he doesn't *hate* them, just thinks that making things up has no point. He doesn't like games, either, unless they're for a practical purpose, for learning or teaching."

"Tyron's the type to make history, not to watch plays about it later," Connor agreed.

"So he'd think this a waste of time, is that it?" Wren asked.

Connor shrugged, and Wren sensed his embarrassment. "If I fail, I'd as soon not have everyone knowing about it," he said finally.

"Well, your secret's safe with me." Wren thought a little, then added tentatively, "Mind if I suggest some ideas now and then?"

Connor laughed. "Suggest anything you want."

Time passed quickly as they compared notes on the few real facts known about the famed magician Tre Resdir. Wren's reading had been in the magical histories, but Connor had gotten his information from the heraldry archives.

It was midafternoon when a neat formation of blue-tunicked Rhismordith equerries appeared behind them. They rode by at a brisk trot, led by a tall, brawny man with a thick red beard. The leader's eyes scanned the travelers on foot. Connor and Wren watched him from the safety of a thick shrub.

When the riders had passed by, Connor said, "You see? They *are* searching. Messengers ride in pairs, not squads, and at a gallop."

Wren nodded. "So we stick with jumping into the bushes every time someone comes. Can't we find any that don't have swarms of bugs?"

Connor only laughed, and they picked up their pace a little, Connor reading from his play as they walked.

Late in the afternoon they heard the rhythmic pounding of horses' hooves coming back toward them from the west.

Until now, they'd paid little heed to travelers coming from the opposite direction. But this sounded like the squad of Blues who had overtaken them earlier.

Connor said, "I think we had better hide."

Resigned, Wren hefted her pack and followed him across a little ditch and behind a screen of low trees.

The hooves got louder. Dust rose just beyond the next bend—and then a neat formation of blue-tunicked equerries rode into view. This time all of them were scanning the roadside. Instinctively both Wren and Connor crouched down—though the trees already hid them from view.

When Wren recognized the foremost rider's red beard, her heart began to pound. "It's the same ones," she said in a low voice when the riders were out of sight. "What does *that* mean?"

"It means they decided they went too far and are retracing their steps."

"That's what I was afraid of," Wren said. "Beginning to look like it's really us, isn't it? What do we do now?"

Connor rubbed his eyes thoughtfully. "I think we're better off taking our chances with the forest road. Maybe we're far enough north to have missed the brigands. They can't be all over the forest; my guess is they lie in wait just outside of Riverfall. We should be safe enough."

Wren hesitated, then thought of Garian's taunts and cruel laughter. Whatever he was up to couldn't be good. And if it were Connor's uncle, the Duke, who was after them . . .

She nodded. "All right. Let's try the forest."

"And we'd better talk about the play later," Connor said, thrusting his papers back into his knapsack.

"Very well," Wren said reluctantly. "But I still think you ought to put in some really terrible weather—like that storm yesterday. That will make the wizards' trip seem all the more real."

"Perhaps you are right."

They struck out directly northward, Connor spotting and following a winding deer trail. "The forest animals will let us know of any humans who are around before we actually see them," Connor said.

"Good," Wren said. "Listen away—I won't talk."

She had never watched him communicating with animals up close, and she was intensely curious to see how it worked. She hoped some good-sized creature would come along.

But nothing—four footed or two—disturbed them during their long late-afternoon walk. They stopped just before sunset and carefully divided the last of the food, saving a portion for morning. Then Connor found them a clearing surrounded by low bushes in which to spend the night. By this time Wren could scarcely see, and her feet were so tired she didn't feel she could take another step. They talked very little as they pulled their cloaks out of their packs and wrapped up in them.

Wren lay back with her head pillowed on her knapsack, looking sleepily up at the stars through the tossing black leaves . . .

. . . and woke up when something sharp prodded her cheek.

"Uhn . . ." she muttered, her dream about Tess and the old orphanage splintering. "Huh?"

She opened her eyes and saw a coldly gleaming spear point. A coarse laugh brought her gaze up to a tall, badly dressed fellow with a filthy beard. He prodded her again with the spear, laughing.

Wren stared in horror. The man had a nasty grin with two missing teeth. "On yer feet, missie," he snarled. "Let's see what's in that pack."

A quick glance showed Connor also lying flat, his head on his pack. Two men and a woman stood nearby, menacing him with spears and a club. His hands were open. *Where was his staff? Had they gotten it, or—*

She glimpsed the end of it under the bush near his feet, less than an arm's length from his hand. He'd hidden it from sight.

She screamed suddenly, and all eyes turned to her. The man with the spear jerked nervously, then brought the butt of his spear down toward her head. She rolled away.

Crack! Connor was on his feet, swinging the staff in a whirling arc. One of the men cried out when his spear went sailing off into the bushes. The staff whanged on the hand of the man with the club, then its butt forced him back into the

69

woman. They staggered. Connor swept the staff under the woman's feet, and she and her crony fell heavily in a tangle of arms and legs, both cursing angrily.

Wren's assailant rushed to help, his hands shifting grip purposefully on the spear. Before he'd taken more than five steps, though, the man stopped suddenly, a fearful noise escaping from his throat as he looked at the trees.

Three terrible monster faces with big red eyes and warty green noses peered out from behind the trees, fanged mouths glistening. Wren squinted at them, concentrating on making the illusions seem real.

"What's that?" The man pointed.

"Yow!" one of the others yelled, and the robbers took to their heels through the bushes, leaving the club and one of the spears behind. The monsters winkled out of existence.

"Thank goodness they don't seem to know about illusions!" Wren exclaimed. "That was good work with the staff," she added admiringly.

"Good work on your own part," Connor replied. "Your illusion saved me. The bearded fellow held his spear like he knows staff work, and I don't think I could have fought him *and* his pals off."

"Then let's get out of here before they figure out those monsters aren't coming after them."

They picked up their packs, and Wren paused to grab the spear from the bushes. Then they hurried through the trees in the direction opposite from that the robbers had taken.

"I hope taking the forest road wasn't a stupid idea," Wren said a little while later. She was panting.

"Here's a stream," Connor replied. "Let's stop long enough to get a drink." He led the way past some close-growing willows to a wide brook.

"Think they're after us?" Wren asked, perching uneasily on a rock.

Connor sat still for a long moment, then he shook his head. "No," he said. "I can hear some broadwing hawk nestlings cheeping down that way." He pointed. "And if a lot of humans were chasing about, they'd be silent and the parent would be giving the warning cry."

"Did you get any warnings, animal or otherwise, before those robbers sneaked up on us?"

"No." Connor looked slightly embarrassed. "I heard one of the brigands rustling through that bush a moment before they were on us. It gave me just enough time to cover my staff. I suspect the local wildlife escaped while we were asleep."

Wren sighed. "Do you think we should go back to the road and risk your relatives? At least they won't be using clubs and spears!"

"We're near the mountains, which means the road is going to be bending toward the northeast."

"And we need to go northwest," Wren said, consulting the map she'd sketched in her book.

"If we stick with pathways going northwest, maybe we can make the border by nightfall. Shall we try?"

Wren scanned her surroundings. The broad maple leaves overhead moved peacefully in the breeze; beyond, the early-morning sky smiled. "Well, I still have my magic, plus this spear—though I don't really know what I'd do with it besides wave it about," she said. "All right. Let's push on."

She bent to get a drink of water, then they picked up their packs and the weapons, and they left.

Chapter Eight

*W*hile Wren and Connor made their way up a difficult mountain path toward the border, back in Cantirmoor, Princess Teressa Rhisadel went down the stairs to face the perils of a formal court dinner.

She had dressed with great care, turning around and around before her mirror to inspect herself from every side. She wanted to make certain that her relatives would have nothing to complain of—and she chose a peach-colored gown with very little trim to make her appearance as unobtrusive as possible.

Her parents walked just in front of her, talking softly. They seemed preoccupied. Teressa knew there had been more trouble that day, this time between two barons who had never caused problems before. But there was nothing she could do to help.

There will be dancing after this awful state dinner, Teressa reminded herself as she followed her parents into the huge dining room.

As soon as they passed through the door, Teressa felt a change in atmosphere. The room looked as it always did— bright candles, pretty tapestries, and people dressed in their best clothes smiling and bowing. But here and there Teressa saw a tight-clenched jaw or fingers gripped hard on a fan. *It feels like the air just before a thunderstorm.* She looked at her parents, but they were nodding and smiling as though nothing were amiss as they made their way to the head table.

Her heart sank when the steward seated her at the end of the table opposite from the King and Queen, right next to Aunt Carlas. This being a formal dinner for only those of very high rank, there was only one table, with adults and young people mixed together. Mirlee sat across from Teressa, and Garian sat three seats up—but at least only two of his friends, Perd and Hawk, were with him. As the boys sat down, Teressa overheard Garian telling one of the adults that Marit wouldn't be coming because he was sick.

After the toast to the King and Queen, food was served. Teressa knew that the evening would be a difficult one when Mirlee, in a failing voice, began criticizing every dish offered by the silent servants.

"Oh, Mirlee." Aunt Carlas gave a sigh. "You are so delicate. What are we to do?"

Stop her from wolfing down so many sweets right before dinner, Teressa thought, looking away from Mirlee's disagreeable expression.

Garian said, "Mirlee, if you won't have that fish cake, pass it over to Perd here."

"Why?" Mirlee sidled a glance at her mother, who was now engaged in conversation with the Baroness Tamsal, then she made a mean face. "Looks to me like Perd's had a few too many fish cakes already," she sneered.

The plump Perd blushed, his eyes wide with hurt and surprise, and without thinking, Teressa said, "It's a mystery to me how a girl with a stomach full of sweets can be so sour."

Several of the girls looked down or at each other, obviously repressing laughs, but Garian and Perd snickered, and Hawk smiled.

Mirlee gasped, anger spots marking her sallow cheeks.

"Young ladies. Young gentlemen," Aunt Carlas said with lofty reproof. She glanced once at Teressa, her pale eyes full of poison. Teressa knew then that her aunt had heard the whole exchange—including Mirlee's part, which was why the reproof was not aimed specifically at Teressa.

Relieved, Teressa turned her attention back to her food. Before long, though, she realized that Aunt Carlas would not reprove her directly, but a far worse punishment lay in store.

As the dinner progressed, Aunt Carlas led the general conversation. From time to time she made pointed comments in her languid voice about breeding, taste, and training. Even Garian and his friends sobered, and what conversation the young people made was stilted and forced.

In the smoothest possible way, the Duchess guided the conversation around to art, and then she mentioned the new mosaic by the carpenters' guildhall. It had been a gift from two barons—one of whom was Marit's father.

"Don't you think the new mosaic is dreadful, cousin?" Mirlee asked, smirking openly.

Teressa bit her lip. No matter what she said, it would be the wrong answer, for the truth was she thought the mosaic ugly, and she knew that most of the court agreed. Except, of course, for Marit and his father. And even though Marit was not present at the dinner, whatever she said would probably be reported back to him.

She looked down at her hands. "It's very handsome," she said in a low voice.

Aunt Carlas favored her with a thin smile. "It is a true shame," she said pityingly, "when children of good birth are raised in a vulgar environment—"

"Such as an orphanage?" Mirlee cut in.

The Duchess sighed. "Regrettable, how it breeds a lack of taste."

Silence met this remark, and Teressa saw several people glance at her, then away. She dropped her napkin, got up, and walked out.

Tears of anger blurred her eyes. She stumbled over the top step on the terrace beyond the dining room. Grabbing up her skirts, she ran to the garden, which was lit by Big

Moon high in the sky and the rising Little Moon, until the cool night air dried her tears.

When she had calmed down, she walked slowly along the pathways, glad to be alone. Despite the darkness, she knew the way to her favorite place, a secluded grotto beside a little stream. She pushed past the thick curtain of willow leaves and dropped down onto the marble bench, starting up again when she heard the crunch of footfalls on the leafy path.

"Tess," a quiet male voice said.

"Father!" Surprised and pleased, Teressa sprang to her feet.

She could not see his expression in the moon's light, but she did not hear anger in his voice as he said, "I thought I might find you here."

"I had to leave for a little while," Teressa said. "It was so hot—"

"Your aunt," the King said gently, "sought me out as soon as the dinner ended."

Teressa winced. "Then you must be angry with me."

"I am angry," he said, "though not with you. Sit down. Tell me what happened."

Teressa joined her father on the bench. He listened in silence while she described the events at dinner. She told her story as truthfully as she knew how, not sparing her own spiteful comment to Mirlee.

He did not speak until she had finished. When he did, his voice was humorous as he said, "That, I need hardly say, scarcely matches your aunt's view of the events."

Stung, Teressa blurted, "You can ask anyone. Even Garian, who at least usually tells the truth—"

"I don't need to ask anyone," her father said. "I am well aware of Carlas's ability to bend the truth as she sees fit. The important thing . . ." Her father hesitated, then reached to take her hand. Holding it in a light, warm clasp, he said, "I think it has been hard for you, being introduced so suddenly to the ways of court after your years with your aunt Leila at that orphanage. Both your mother and I think you've adjusted extremely well," he hastened to add.

"I've tried," Teressa said.

"I know," he responded. "In fact, you've tried so hard, and done so well, that we sometimes forget—we'd like to forget—that you weren't always with us. But at the same time, we don't know you as well as we might, had you been able to grow up here with us."

Teressa bit her lip. She had rarely admitted even to herself that her parents often seemed like strangers to her.

"You always work hard, and you never complain," the King continued. "But we never really know what you are thinking and feeling."

"I thought that was part of being a princess," Teressa said. "Hiding your real thoughts. Being polite."

"That's part of it," her father agreed. "Though I hope you do not think you need to hide your true feelings from us."

If this conversation had taken place in daylight, Teressa might have remained silent, but somehow the darkness made it feel safe to answer. "You and Mother are always polite," she said. "To everyone. Even to me. So I can't tell what *you* are thinking, including about me."

"True," her father said. "We are so adept at the court mask that we sometimes find it difficult to be ourselves, even when we are alone. And we have been careful with you this past year, not because we doubted you, but because we wanted you to have the chance to get to know court life before you began the difficult lessons that face a ruler."

"I don't mind court so much, except for Aunt Carlas and Garian and Mirlee. Aunt Carlas *hates* me!" Teressa exclaimed. "I know she wishes I had never come back so that Garian could have my place."

"Your first lesson," the King said, taking both her hands in a firm grip. "Some truths must never go beyond our family circle. Even if Andreus had killed you as he threatened, I

76

never would have selected Garian as my heir. You can remind yourself of that from time to time, if it will help."

Teressa could hear his smile in his voice. She sighed.

"And here's the second part of that lesson," the King went on. "It doesn't matter who was right and who wrong at that dinner tonight. The fact is, Mirlee and Carlas are not going to change, and they are not going to go away. When you become queen, you *must* be able to get along with people like them, or your court will be divided—and open to attack from outside."

He doesn't like them either, Teressa thought.

"All these social events are practice for the future," her father went on. "You can be a weak queen and hide from the people you don't like. Then your advisers will be the real rulers, and I hope you'll have chosen good advisers." He laughed a little. "Or—"

"Or I learn to be a strong queen," Teressa said. "But how?"

"One thing that helped me was to think of court life as a kind of game," her father said.

"But that's what Andreus said to me," Teressa protested, troubled. "He said everything was just a game."

"I suspect we look at games differently, then," the King said. "To Andreus, the goal is to win at the expense of all other players. To me, the object is to make everyone a winner, even those who are not aware of the game."

"I think . . . I see," Teressa said.

"I thought you would." Her father leaned forward to kiss her on the forehead. "I'd better get back now, before someone notices how long I've been gone. Want to come back with me and join the dancing?"

"I'd like to stay here a bit and think this through," she said. "But I will be there soon."

"Good. And always remember: we love you very much." The King got up and left the grotto, walking swiftly up the pathway.

Teressa followed more slowly, thinking through what her father had told her. She realized that the distance she had perceived from her parents had actually been a kind of protection. *They have been hiding all the important bad things from me until I learn how to deal with the small stuff—like Mirlee.* She stopped, looking up the pathway toward the palace. *I've got to stop thinking of these state events as chores and see them instead as challenges.*

She was startled out of her thoughts when she became aware of running footsteps on the pathway behind her. Holding her wide skirts to keep them from rustling against the shrubs, she stepped off the path behind a huge elm.

A glow-globe had been hung in a little clearing a few steps beyond, where two paths intersected. Teressa saw Garian's friend Marit running up the path, with frequent glances behind him.

Wasn't he supposed to be sick? Teressa thought as he disappeared along an adjacent pathway.

She looked down at her skirts. Chasing after the long-legged Marit in those would be impossible. *Maybe I won't have to,* she thought, looking at the path he'd taken, which led by a winding route to the family wing of the palace. *Because I know a shortcut.*

She hurried down a narrow, overgrown side route that she and Wren had discovered while searching for secret paths.

She was breathing hard when she neared the palace. Stopping in the lee of an overhanging shrub, she was just in time to see Marit step out of the garden, look around, then dash into the secluded rock garden just off the palace's Sunset Terrace.

Her slippers skimming lightly over the smooth flagstones, Teressa followed him. She veered at the last moment when she remembered a secret entrance to the garden at the back, shaded by an old willow.

She reached the willow quickly and peered into the rock garden, which was partially illuminated by the lanterns high on the terrace wall. Just then Garian and Perd Ambur pounded in at a dead run, breathless and looking scared.

As soon as he saw them, Marit yelled, "It works! It works! I never half believed any of that magic stuff really worked—" He held up one hand, on which a ring with a glowing blue stone flashed.

"Keep your voice down, haybrain," Garian snarled. Teressa saw a glow of blue on Garian's hand as well. Pointing at his ring, he said, "So why did you do the summons spell?"

Marit lowered his voice slightly. "You were right. The King's steward lied—Lackland *is* at liberty, and he's traveling with Wren, the magic prentice who saved Princess Teressa last year. My stepbrother didn't actually see them, but he asked at some inns, and the descriptions matched."

Garian squawked even louder than Marit. "He *missed* them?"

"Well, you *know* the Blues are not really soldiers, they're messengers," Perd put in defensively. "If you want to call out the family guard—"

"Sure, and have to explain it to my father?"

Marit said, "Let's go find them ourselves. What fun!"

"I'm still confined to this blasted palace, dolt!" Garian snapped. Then he stamped around in a circle, muttering, "Wait. Shut up—let me think. The Blues have *got* to grab them. They've got to. Let's go get Hawk, and we'll plan."

All three of them hurried out of the garden.

Wren's in danger, Teressa thought. And then a cold hand seemed to grip her inside. *Can these boys be somehow mixed up with the troubles here in Cantirmoor?*

I've got to tell my father!

She plunged back through the shrubs, pausing to brush the leaves off her skirt before she entered the palace from a seldom-used side door. Then she made her way to the ballroom, only to stop in dismay when she saw the crowd of figures moving gracefully to music.

In the very center of the ballroom were her parents, each dancing with an important court figure. She knew if she went up to them and interrupted, there would be avid eavesdroppers on all sides. She supposed she should wait, but she felt the urge to talk it out with someone right away.

So whom do I tell? she thought, looking around.

Her eyes traveled from the glittering dancers to the musicians high in the gallery. All the foremost aristocrats of Meldrith were in the room—and Teressa couldn't be sure which of them might be part of Garian's plot. Who was safe to talk to?

At that moment a flicker of white caught the edge of her vision. She turned, saw a familiar tall, thin figure in the formal white tunic of the magicians. Tyron! He was just sitting down near a group of gossiping minor courtiers who looked at him once, then ignored him. His face was set in an expression of unmistakable boredom.

Stifling the desire to laugh, Teressa wandered toward him and paused beside a refreshment table. She picked up a crystal cup filled with punch. Drinking it off quickly, she set it down so the crystal rang on the table.

The sound carried a little way over the music. Tyron looked up, and Teressa lifted her hand just a little.

Tyron's face changed from boredom to interest, then smoothed out almost at once. He got up and made his way toward her, executed a creditable bow, then reached to fill a cup with punch.

Teressa grasped another ladle, allowing her hair to fall forward to screen her face. "Meet me in the Rainbow Room," she whispered. "I heard something—Garian—about Connor and Wren."

Tyron's eyes widened, but he said nothing. He made his way back to his chair, and Teressa glided along the perimeter of the ballroom in the other direction, nodding serenely this way and that as people bowed to her. Eventually she reached the hallway leading to the smaller salons used as anterooms during formal court sessions.

A few people strolled the halls, mostly in twos and threes, heading to and from the terrace.

Teressa waited for a space between wanderers, then slipped into the room. She scarcely looked at the sudden glory of the mosaic made from Rainbow Lake stones. Candles burning in sconces played over the gemlike stones, making them glitter. She'd picked this room because it had only one door and because she happened to know that it had a mighty spell on it against eavesdroppers. Silently she sat down on the brocaded couch.

Tyron did not keep her waiting long. He opened the door, shut it firmly behind him, then hurried to the couch.

"Well, that sure woke me up," he said, dropping onto a chair with a sigh of relief. "What's this about Wren and Connor? Not trouble, I hope?"

Teressa nodded. "I think so. I'll tell my parents just as soon as I can get them alone."

"That won't be until dawn," Tyron said practically. "That's the horror of these things—they go on all night."

"Don't like balls, do you?"

Tyron made a terrible face. "If I'd known that this dancing stuff would be part of my job, I'd have thought twice about serving as Halfrid's heir," he joked, then immediately turned serious. "So what have you heard?"

Teressa got up and moved to the door. She threw the latch, then turned to face Tyron. "I think I'd better start from dinner, when I—well, I decided to leave early and get some air."

Tyron's brows lifted, then he gave her a conspiratorial grin.

Teressa smiled back a little. "Was my defeat so obvious, then?"

Tyron waved a hand. "I didn't see you until you got up. And then I noticed you had been sitting next to Duchess Carlas and her poison-piece of a daughter. What happened was easy enough to guess, if you don't mind my plain speaking about your relatives."

"I don't mind at all," she said. "Though I think I've learned something since. Anyway, I was walking about afterward, when . . ."

She went on to describe Marit's trip through the garden.

When she got to the glowing rings, Tyron jerked upright on his chair. "Summons rings," he exclaimed. "Wonder where they got *those?* They're fearsomely difficult to make, and the King frowns on that kind of thing, Halfrid told me."

"You'll have to tell me how they work," Teressa said. "Anyway . . ." She described the remainder of the conversation.

"Lackland," Tyron said, frowning. "I hate that. I know it bothers Connor, though he's never said."

"It's the fashion now for those who will inherit titles to call each other by them," Teressa said. "And of course anyone who won't inherit anything gets a nickname like Lackland."

"What a gang," Tyron said, holding his nose and waving a hand. "Just think! Someday it's going to be my job to protect 'em all by magic, and yours to protect 'em by rule."

Teressa laughed. "What a *lovely* thought. But just now our immediate problem . . ."

"All right. Let me think. Planning with Hawk—Hawk." Tyron pursed his lips. "I've only seen him once, from a distance. He only seems to come to the big court functions, and then Garian and his friends always stay well away from the foul air around such lowborn folks as, for instance, myself." He sniffed his sleeve elaborately.

Teressa laughed.

Tyron's face went serious. "Where does he come from? He's not a local, is he?"

Teressa shook her head. "He's a foreigner, at court to get practice in diplomacy. That's what Uncle Fortian told us. He inherited a huge property down south in the Brennic Marches or Fil Gaen or some such place, and it's being run by a regent. His letter of introduction from their king was quite legitimate, Father said, and so did Halfrid."

"He certainly targeted the country's biggest pests to make friends with. Great diplomat material."

"Maybe that's what everybody is like where he comes from. But never mind him now. What can we do? I'm stuck here—I can't do *anything* to help." She got up and whirled around, trying to fight the sudden surge of anger that swept through her.

"Well, neither can I," Tyron said practically. "At least, not if you mean riding off sword in hand on a horse to chase Marit Limmeran's brother or Garian's Blues. But you *can* do just what you did now—listen. Want some advice?"

Teressa nodded. "Certainly."

"Go back to that ball. If Garian and his vulture pals have shown up, stay around them as much as you can. Listen to everything they say. I'm going to find Halfrid and Leila— nobody will pay any attention to a bunch of dull magicians talking in a corner." He paused. "Or if they do, maybe that will be something to be noted as well."

"All right, if you'll promise to tell me anything you find out."

"I promise."

Teressa gave a strained-sounding laugh. "Then here I go. Though I'd rather be on that horse waving the sword."

Chapter Nine

A little while later, midway up a rocky mountainside just across the border into Siradayel, Connor was startled when Wren suddenly sat bolt upright. Her face was pale in the blue moonlight.

Reaching for his staff, he said, "What—?"

"Magic." She clapped her hands over her face. "Wait."

Connor sniffed the air, his ears straining. No sounds, no smells—everything seemed peaceful. Still, he gripped his staff, ready to spring to his feet, until Wren sank back with a sigh.

"There. I think that worked," she said.

"What happened?"

"Somebody tried to scry me," she said.

"How do you know?" Connor asked. "What's it like?" Despite his years at the Magic School, he had no idea.

Wren rubbed her eyes and pulled her cloak more closely around her. "Imagine yourself working alone in a room," she said. "Then there's a knock at the door. Only you don't have the room, the door, or the knock. You are alone—and then suddenly you know someone is there, thinking about you. *At* you. So you listen outside yourself."

"Who was it?"

"Well, that's what I don't know. Whoever it was didn't want me to know, either."

"Can you get rid of this spy?"

"I hope so. I haven't had much practice with that kind of scrying trick yet. But I was told to try shutting a door in my mind, to close the other scryer out. That's what I did, but it's hard not to try to peek, to see if it—or they—are really gone." Wren yawned, then rubbed her eyes again, her movements brisk in the darkness. "Little Moon's halfway across the sky—isn't it my turn to watch? I'm plenty awake now."

"If you like." Connor pulled his cloak from his knapsack and wrapped up in it. Finding a flat spot with long, soft grass, he stretched out on his back, staring up at the brilliant canopy of multicolored stars. *Who is after us? And why?*

He was just closing his eyes at last when Wren stifled an exclamation, then scrambled for her knapsack.

Connor flung off his cloak and reached for his staff.

"It's happening again," Wren muttered. "But this time it's Mistress Leila—I can see her clear as anything. Where's my stone?" She scrabbled in her knapsack. "I just hope this works . . ." She pulled the stone out and quickly unwrapped it. "If you want to hear, then hold on to me," Wren said, and Connor reached out to grasp Wren's hand. He watched the egg-sized stone that sat on her other palm. It reflected the stars in tiny pinpoints.

A flicker deep inside the stone glowed with blue-white light, and suddenly Connor saw his sister Leila's face.

"Get to Pelsir as fast as you can, and *wait*," Leila commanded. "It's safe—protected by both border guards and very old magic. We'll send either someone or another message to you, as fast as we can."

"Why?" Wren sounded cheerful and confident. "If we run into trouble while I'm on my quest, I do know the Transportation spell. Though I don't want to come home unless I have to—"

"You *can't* come home," Leila cut in. "That's why I am sending right now, at risk of being overheard. There is an accomplished sorcerer who seems to want one—or both—of you, a sorcerer strong enough to have tainted the Transportation Designations here at the school and at the palace. We can't reach you by magic, and you must not try to transport home. You will never arrive."

Her image winked out.

Wren sighed. "I meant to tell her that those Blues are chasing us, sent by Garian. Do you think I should try to raise her again? Maybe they could corner him and find out if he's with this sorcerer. After all, how did he find out where we are?"

Connor shrugged. "Garian would just deny it, whether he is in league with the sorcerer or not. They're going to have to trap the sorcerer some other way."

"Then that's that," Wren said, wrapping up the stone and putting it away. "Looks like we're on our own."

"Let me go find them, at least," Tyron was saying to Halfrid back in the Cantirmoor Magic School as Wren put away her scry-stone.

Tyron moved restlessly to the window and pounded his fist on the sill. "Even if we can't transport them back, why can't I just ride outside the city, scry them, and transport to them?"

"That's three dangerous operations," Halfrid said calmly. "It would almost be better if you risked the Transportation spell from here—"

"Then I will!"

"—and you'll end up, if you transfer at all, in some other world. I tell you that whatever binds our Destination is a comprehensive spell, and it will take us some time to unravel."

"But they're *alone* up there, Wren and Connor. We can't just sit here—*I* just can't sit here and do nothing." Tyron groaned and slammed his palm against the back of a chair. "Why didn't I just drop everything and go with them when I had the chance?"

"Because we've sent them *out* of danger, not *into* it,"

86

Halfrid said. "We can't reach them by transport magic, but they will be safe enough in Pelsir. Meanwhile, the Designation magic was ruined right here in Cantirmoor, which means the sorcerer is in the city. We must solve the problem from here."

"If this cursed magician stays in Cantirmoor and doesn't hare off into the mountains to chase them. I still can't forget what happened to Wren, and it makes me suspicious that the Designation gets ruined when they are gone."

"If that occurs, we do have allies we can call upon to intervene. And Wren and Connor are not completely without resources," Halfrid noted.

"More so, maybe, than we have been led to believe," said a new voice.

Tyron whirled around to see Mistress Leila enter the room.

Halfrid raised an eyebrow. "I take it you are referring to Connor?"

Have they somehow found out Connor's secret? Tyron thought. *I know he hasn't told anyone but Wren, Teressa, and me.*

Mistress Leila nodded, her heavy red braid touched with golden highlights by the streaming candle flames. "I've been convinced for a long time that my little half-brother would surprise us all."

"So you said when you first brought him to us as a prospective magic student." Halfrid sat back in his chair, lacing his hands comfortably over his round middle. "Perhaps you are right. We shall see, shall we not? But what we need to find out right now is who is causing the problems here in Cantirmoor. The King said he's never seen the like, not even in the bad old days when his grandfather and old uncle nearly split the country with their squabbling."

Tyron said, "I've tried. But I haven't been able to figure out who's behind it."

Mistress Leila gave him a wintry smile. "Before you blame yourself for the problems of the entire court, you ought to compare observations with the rest of us."

"What do you mean?" Halfrid asked, sitting forward again.

"Only this: It seems odd that every single untoward thing that has occurred has happened when *we* have not been present. When *we* attend court functions, nothing happens beyond the ordinary."

Tyron thought hard. "That's right—I'd gone home early the day Flord and Jamery had that fight—"

"And the near-duel between Baron Lianac and that visiting prince from Allat Los happened the day the Queen and I went to visit Maressa and her new baby," Leila put in.

"And the two open Council meetings I missed were on days that contentious questions were introduced, always by someone unknown . . ." Halfrid said musingly.

"Suggests someone doesn't want magicians around, doesn't it?" Mistress Leila said.

"Our first proof—if you can call it proof—that the troubles besetting court and the peculiar difficulties with this magician may actually be tied together," Halfrid said, stroking his white beard. "Hmmm . . ."

Tyron went back to the window, wishing once again he could talk to Wren and Connor. If he were a bird, say, he could fly across the mountains and—

Turning suddenly to face his seniors, he said, "I think I know what can be done."

They looked up at him.

"You won't like it."

"We'll be the judges of that," Mistress Leila said.

"You'll say it's dangerous and crazy and foolhardy—"

"Give over, then, my boy," Halfrid said, with a ghost of a chuckle.

"But *Wren* would say, 'If *I* can do it, anyone can.' "

Mistress Leila pursed her lips and Halfrid's white eyebrows rose. "Keep talking," he invited.

When her scry-stone was safely stowed in the bag, Wren waited for some kind of comment from Connor. Instead he sat there, his head bowed. She could not see his face in the darkness, so she had no clue to his thoughts.

"Connor?"

His head came up. "So that's what scrying feels like," he said. "I've felt that before. Yesterday. The day of the storm. And just a while ago."

Wren whistled softly. "Really? Who was scrying you?"

"I don't know. I just had that same feeling, like someone was with me inside my head. Only then it came with a sense of danger. Each time I looked around, saw no one, and then thrust the matter out of my mind. Eventually the feeling vanished and I thought no more of it."

"Then you must have somehow managed to do the door-closing thing naturally," Wren said. "Didn't they teach you about scrying when you were a magic student?"

"I never made it that far," Connor said.

"They didn't test you?"

"Had me look into a stone once. Nothing happened. And I never felt that feeling before, at least not when I was a student. The first time was after the storm—no," he amended, his voice reflective. "The first time was last year, when we were in the mountains outside Senna Lirwan. I felt we were being watched almost the entire time we were flying on the chrauchans, but it was a *reassuring* feeling. I don't know quite how to explain it. Anyway, so much happened to us afterward, I quite forgot about it until now."

"The Sendimerys twins were scrying us when we flew through the mountains. Tyron told me that later. So you felt them—and neither Tyron nor I did. Now, *that's* a strange thing."

Connor shrugged.

"I can't figure it out," Wren said. "You can't do magic, but you can feel someone scrying you—and close it off."

Connor shrugged again, his expression unreadable in the moonlight. "It doesn't make sense to me, either, any more than it makes sense that I can communicate with animals when I touch them. All animals. Except birds—with them all I have to do is see them to know their thoughts."

"I'll tell you one thing," Wren said, "if you didn't get rid of this sneezeweed of a magician right away, then the sneezeweed has figured out where we are." Her hands dove into her pack. "I'd better scry—no! I can't."

Connor nodded. "If you do, we risk being overheard, right?"

"Right. And anyway, what can they do? They can't come to us, and we can't go to them."

"Right," Connor said, rising to his feet. "Let's get moving to Pelsir."

Wren shivered, grabbed her belongings, and they strode uphill toward the dark western mountain peaks.

Connor spotted the first sign of trouble almost right away, and only because of his gift. As they toiled up the trail at their fastest, Connor listened out of habit for any other signs of life, human or otherwise.

When he sensed the spybird, the evil intent in its mind startled him. Without thinking he put out a hand and grabbed Wren by the collar. She promptly ducked at once under a low, thick-growing shrub.

Connor dropped beside her and shut his eyes, listening with that mysterious inner sense until the bird passed beyond a far mountain peak.

When he opened his eyes, Wren's moonlit form was waiting nearby.

"Well?" she said, just a little sharply.

"I'm sorry I grabbed you like that. It was a spybird, and someone was using it . . . oh, like that scrying business," Connor said, struggling for the right words. "I don't know quite how to explain it."

"Bad magic." Wren's tone changed. "I heard that some magicians can put an enchantment on other creatures, then look through their eyes with their scry-stones, in order to see what they see. Supposedly, really mighty sorcerers—like the Emperor of Sveran Djur—can do it to people, not just to animals, but that might just be fireside talk."

The idea of that made Connor's skin crawl. He shook himself, then said, "We'd better make speed, then. This sorcerer knows the general area we are in, which must mean searchers are on the way."

Wren hefted her knapsack and they set out again, both keeping careful watch, not just around them, but also on the skies above.

A short time later they scrambled over the top of an especially steep rise, then stopped to stare at the huge fortress sitting atop a big mountain to the west, glowing with countless dots of ruddy firelight.

"That's it," Connor said, trying to catch his breath. "Pelsir."

"Safety," Wren added. "All we have to do is get down this mountain and up the next one in order to reach it."

Connor stared through the airy distance. The sense of magic in the mountains was strong, so strong that it gave him a peculiar sense of weightlessness. As if he could just stretch out his arms, leap off this cliff—and fly.

A moment of vertigo overtook him. He felt unsteady, as if his feet were already moving toward the cliff edge. He stumbled back, fear freezing his thoughts.

"Connor?" Wren's voice was sharp with sudden worry.

"Nothing," he said. "I think we'd better get going."

"Fog coming." Wren pointed back toward the east. "Slows us up a little, but it will also slow anyone looking for us."

"Good."

They found a narrow animal trail and started down, soon losing themselves in a thick forest of tall conifers. They walked in silence. Fog had begun to obscure the treetops when Connor, glancing up, saw a strange glow reflecting off the mist.

91

"Wren—look!"

Almost as soon as he said it, the glowing thing cleared a wisp of fog and drifted into view. Terror struck at Connor when he saw a huge serpent-shape drift through the branches directly above their path. "What is that?"

"Oh!" Wren gasped—in relief.

Before Connor could question, she brought her hands up, muttered something, and pointed, and the floating serpent disappeared with a silent *pop*.

"It was only an illusion." Wren's voice sounded shaky. "But it still scared me—oh, *no!*"

Coldness gripped Connor inside. "And now whoever made it knows exactly where we are, because only a magician could pop it."

"Oh, I'm *sorry*." Wren groaned. "I didn't think of that. I guess I was still worried about spybirds—"

"Let's get out of here," Connor said.

They began to run, heedless of the branches slapping their faces, the rocks causing them to stumble and slide. Connor led the way, Wren following close behind, her head down and her breathing harsh. She stumbled once, falling over her spear. When she got up, she left it behind.

The attack, when it came, was sudden.

They heard it before they saw it. A weird *whoosh*ing noise swept suddenly overhead; a strange wind tore through the treetops. Skidding to a stop, they looked upward.

What they saw was worse than a wind: the evil red glow of fire, leaping from tree to tree with the speed of inexorable magic.

Wren let out a cry.

Connor whirled around. "Come on!" he yelled, fighting his way back up the trail.

"Why? Where?" Wren gasped behind him, her voice nearly drowned by the roar and crackle above them.

Hot cinders rained down around them, but Connor did not veer. *Up*, a voice inside commanded. It was a familiar voice, one he hadn't heard in a very long time, but he did not stop to question or identify. He ran harder, even though he could hear Wren, whose stride was so much shorter, lagging behind—and he could hear the panic cries and noises of the fleeing forest animals.

He ran until his lungs hurt, at last emerging from the trees onto another cliff nearly as high as the last.

Wren appeared a moment later and fell flat on the ground. "Fire!" she cried. "Living creatures . . . in that forest."

Connor dropped his gear, stumbling dizzily against a huge, moss-covered boulder and wincing at the sounds of distress coming so clearly to him now. "Animals . . ." He sucked in a shuddering breath. "Animals . . . birds. Running . . . but not fast enough."

Forcing himself to look, he saw the entire mountainside engulfed in sheets of flame. The fire glowed strangely through the banks of fog still drifting through the air.

Fog . . . not enough moisture to help against a fire. All those lives, caught—helpless—What can be done?

Wren was already scrabbling through her knapsack. She pulled out her book, her fingers shaking. "I don't know enough magic for this," she muttered. "But I have to try, I have to try."

Connor watched, his body tense and still. She snapped her fingers, and a tiny witch-light appeared above her book. Her finger fumbled through the closely written pages, then she raised one hand and made a pass, mumbling spell words all the while. A weak flash of bluish light a little way down the mountainside dissolved a small spot of flame, leaving blackness that almost immediately filled with fire again.

"I can't do it," Wren said, her voice quavering. "I just don't know enough. It needs a *big* spell."

A big spell, indeed, Connor thought, his eyes on the distant horizon. But not the kind of magic that Wren was learning, the kind that went sideways for Connor. There was something else, something that drew on the tingling feeling that the distant snowy peaks and the scattered stars caused in him. Something that had no words or signs, but that he *felt*—

Don't you feel the magic? Gather it to you, came a voice.

He knew that voice speaking through memory now, though he hadn't heard it aloud in ten years: his father, talking to him when Connor was very small. Connor was standing, shivering violently, on a snowy cliff beside his father. *Reach with your mind and gather it,* his father had said. *Into your hands.*

Connor shut his eyes, *seeing* the vast, glittering light-magic . . .

Reaching with his mind he swept the skies, gathering to him all the light until he felt his palms begin to burn.

Gather it, then focus it and release it. All at once. And fast, or it will take you with it . . .

He sucked in a breath and turned his eyes to the fog, imagining towering clouds, and then he brought his hands together—how slow they were!—in one clap.

Thunder rocked the cliffside, sending lightning ripping through the sky. A moment later steely needles of cold rain stung his face and arms, and he fell down on the ground beside Wren, his cheek grinding into the small sharp stones, his mind whirling dizzily into darkness.

". . . Connor?"

That was Wren.

"Connor, are you all right?"

Connor rolled over. Cold rain beat on his face, running into his clothes. He lifted stone-heavy eyelids. The darkness hid Wren's face, but he could hear her worry in the way she breathed.

"Connor? Please wake up."

He gritted his teeth, sat up. Some of the lassitude slid away, leaving him feeling alive again. But his body ached all over.

"I'm fine." He managed to get the words out.

94

"We've got to go," she said. "People are coming. On horseback, carrying torches. With swords."

A gray shape moved: her arm, pointing down over the cliffside. The rain was soft now, diminishing rapidly. Connor stumbled to his feet, just barely made out the road directly below them.

"They rode right past us," Wren said, "but I wouldn't trust them not to come back. They aren't Blues; they're wearing chain mail and everything."

Who? Where from? Connor shook his head hard, beyond dealing with such questions now. "We've got to get to Pelsir." It sounded like somebody else's voice. Somebody about eight years old and far away.

"Right," Wren agreed. There was a quiet note in her voice, a reflective note. He couldn't think about that, either.

Connor bent to pick up his staff and his knapsack. The ground seemed to be a great distance away.

They started down the mountainside once more, Connor trying to fight the heavy tiredness that pressed on him. He misliked the utter silence of the forest, though it looked as if the damage had been mostly confined to the treetops.

As if she shared his thought, Wren said, "That rainstorm seems to have killed the fire before it took proper hold. But all the animals have fled."

Connor forced himself to speak. "We'll keep away from roads."

They walked for what seemed years, Connor concentrating on putting one foot in front of the other. Once the end of his staff caught in a shrub, ripping from his clumsy fingers and falling to the ground.

He blinked down at it and was tempted just to let it lie, but Wren dove to pick it up.

"I'll carry that," she said. "I lost my spear when we ran from the fire. You just think about walking. It would be good if we could go a bit faster," she added in a careful voice.

Connor shuffled his feet more quickly, a pace that lasted the space of ten steps. Blinking around, he saw Wren's braids swinging as she watched for danger. He realized he could see her features, which meant the sun was coming up at last. Then his mind blanked again, until Wren's voice came sharply:

"We'd better hide—"

"They're here!" A man's shout.

Connor whirled around, his feet tangling in the long grass, and he fell hard. Dizziness overwhelmed him. He shut his eyes, trying to fight it off, and heard the familiar *whoosh* of his staff.

"Don't come any closer!" Wren yelled, clumsily swinging the staff.

Harsh laughter. The crack of steel on wood.

"Ow!" Wren exclaimed, and the staff clattered down beside Connor.

"All right," a man's voice grated. "Now you'll—"

The man was interrupted by a new sound, a *whoosh* and a *thok!* followed by Wren's triumphant "Take *that!*"

Forcing his bleary eyes open, Connor saw Wren swinging her sash around in a fast circle. Using it as a slingshot, she let fly, and a second stone hit a huge armed man square on the nose. He fell back, howling curses, but several other men advanced, a step at a time.

Got to move . . . Got to move . . . Connor gritted his teeth, his hand closing on his staff.

"Next one near us gets one in the eye," Wren yelled.

"Circle 'em," another voice, one with authority, grated.

Connor forced himself to sit up, but the world spun crazily.

Wren's arm began to revolve, but before she let another stone fly another voice rang out: "Drop your weapons, all of you. By order of Queen Nerith of Siradayel!"

My mother. So we've been rescued, and by the Siradi Border Guard. But . . . but . . .

Connor made a great effort and motioned to Wren. She dropped down next to him and he whispered, "Don't tell them who I am."

Then the fog closed in. And silence.

Chapter Ten

*W*ren bit her lip, then knocked on the heavy wooden door.

"Enter." That was Connor, and—relief!—he sounded himself again.

Shifting her bundle under her arm, Wren lifted the latch and pushed the door open. Inside the small, plain room, Connor sat at the window, staring down at the valley far below. Sunrise gleamed in his gray eyes and shone on a face healthy with color.

Remembering how pale his cheeks had been yesterday and how blank those eyes had seemed, Wren repressed a shudder. "Feel better?" she asked as she walked in.

He grinned his old merry grin. "I ought to. I don't think I've ever slept clear through one day and into the next. I take it we are in the Pelsir Fortress?"

"You don't remember the ride?" Wren asked.

He shook his head. "Tell me everything."

Wren dropped onto a small three-legged stool. "Here's your other tunic. Clean. They have a hot spring running through here, lower down. I can show you anytime you like. You can get a great bathe."

"Thanks," he said, taking the roll of clothes.

Wren shrugged, wondering how to broach the subject foremost in her mind. She remembered one of her first lessons with Master Falstan. *There are different ways to shape magic,* he'd said. *Those of us who aren't born with the gift for gathering and using it have to learn the keys and controls. It's a long process, but it's the safest one: The controls protect the magician and the magician's environment. The inborn gifts, such as those inherited by descendants of the Iyon Daiyin, are in one sense easier, but they can be far more dangerous.*

"Where do you want me to start?" She shifted her eyes to the window. "A strange adventure," she added. "I thought *I* was supposed to be the magician, and *you* were to handle any fighting."

"I remember you being pretty knacky with your sash."

"We did a lot of rock slinging when I was in the orphanage, during the times when the river was low. I was always a good aim. Still, it wasn't enough to fight 'em off, and was I glad to see the Pelsir Border Guards! Those villains scuttled away like so many rats in a drain, though I think the Browns might have caught one or two of them." Wren hesitated, then blurted, "Was that Iyon Daiyin magic, there on the mountain?"

He gave his head a quick shake. "I don't know. I've never done it before." His voice was subdued. "And I don't really recall what I did."

Whether he was telling the truth or not, Wren realized he wasn't going to say anything more. She had a vivid image of Connor surrounded by light, his wide eyes reflecting the weird glow as they focused beyond the sky. He'd clapped his hands, the thunder and rain had struck, and then he'd toppled right onto his face in a dead faint. *Dangerous is right.*

She said briskly, "Well, we're safe enough while we're here. But I don't understand why you didn't want them to know who you are. You don't think these people are a threat?"

"Not at all," Connor said. "But we're in Siradayel now—my country. If they find out who I am they'll start bowing and Your-Gracing, and they'd probably feel obliged to force me to go back to Paranir and my mother. For my safety. I'd rather be left to make my own choices, like any ordinary citizen."

"That makes sense," Wren said. "Anyway, I told them your name is Falstan and you're a player's journeyman. It was the fastest thing I could think of."

"Thanks."

Wren went on, "I guess there's a strong chance that whoever sent those toe-molds after us will have some more waiting when we leave."

"Unless we return to Cantirmoor by magic," Connor said.

Wren looked at him in surprise. "You—"

Connor laughed. "Not me! I don't think I'll repeat whatever happened the other night—even if I could." He made a dismissive gesture, then went on, "I was thinking we could somehow send a message to Tyron and have him bring us back. Or my sister Leila, when they get the Designation fixed."

About to refuse, Wren bit her lip. She didn't even know yet whether her quest for information about her parents would produce any clues to follow. It could be they would have to return to Cantirmoor anyway, though the thought filled her with disappointment.

She said, "Well, we have a week to decide what to do. Turns out it costs something to dig in the records, and since I don't want to unpocket my whole store of coins, I'll have to work. They gave me a job in the stable, which frees one of them up for more important things."

"I'll help, if you like," Connor offered.

"Only if you really want to," Wren said. "I started yesterday, and it's great fun. In fact, I have to go down there when the big bell rings, but I want to show you where the breakfast place is."

Connor got promptly to his feet. "The best thing I've heard yet. I think I've forgotten what hot food tastes like."

They walked out into a narrow hall, and Wren said,

"Don't forget where your room is. I'm next door. This is where the guests stay—but all the halls and doors look alike."

She led them swiftly down a stone hallway, past white-washed walls. Glow-globes cast light at intervals; at the stairway, which went down in a spiral, slanting rays bisected the stairs through window slits set in the thick stones.

"This is a real tower," Wren said, her voice echoing. "Can you imagine the games we could have here? I spent most of the evening yesterday wandering around. If I don't make magician, I could have lots of fun being one of these people."

"Along with being a player, and a trader, and—"

"So I like a lot of things," Wren said over her shoulder. "It's lucky I'll probably be a wandering magician, isn't it? Here we are."

They pushed through a door and walked onto a balcony that overlooked a vast courtyard. Towers stood high above the thick crenellated walls, gray against the distant dark mountain peaks.

Opening two massive doors, they entered a refectory noisy with people. They stood in line with several tall young men and women, all of whom wore sturdy brown tunics and thick trousers stuffed into the tops of high riding boots; battered swords and knives hung at their sides. Wren wondered if any of the Browns in the room had been on the rescue mission that had saved her ten years ago, on one of these very peaks. A few looked old enough. Thinking so gave her a peculiar feeling.

She'd just tucked into her breakfast when a great bell tolled four times. The sound seemed to come from everywhere.

People jumped up and scurried in several directions. Wren snatched an extra piece of hot cheese-topped bread from her plate and stuffed it into her mouth. Waving a hasty good-bye to Connor, she raced down to the stable, where she spent a happy morning pitching hay, currying the well-kept mountain ponies, and listening to the gossip of the prentice-aged Browns doing stable duty.

When she went back upstairs at the end of her shift, she found Connor in his room. He was sitting on the floor, his papers propped on the three-legged stool and spread around him on the floor. He was writing.

"Your play," Wren exclaimed.

He blinked up at her, his thoughts obviously far away.

"Your door was open." Wren pointed back over her shoulder. "What part are you at?"

Connor laid his pen down. "I looked it over. There is hardly any mention of weather. One thing I've learned on our trip is that weather is of primary importance. I'd forgotten that. So I've written in a couple of fierce storms."

Wren laughed, her fingers weaving patterns in the air. For a moment illusionary rain fell, blurring the walls. Then she waved and the illusion disappeared in a shower of stars. "That'll be fun for the stage magician," she said. "And have you added anything about brigands on the road?"

Connor shook his head as he swept his papers together. "No—though that's certainly realistic," he said thoughtfully.

"This journey might be the best thing for your play," Wren responded. "As long as we live through it! Whatever happens to us probably happened to Tre Resdir and Morayen. Ready for dinner? I'm starving, and I wouldn't mind company."

Connor readily joined her, but afterward he was reluctant to wander around the fortress with her. Guessing he was afraid someone might recognize him, she left him to return to his play and continued her explorations on her own.

Late the next morning, Wren was pitching soiled hay out of a stall when one of the stable hands tapped her on the shoulder. She put down her pitchfork and looked up in question.

"Watch Commander wants you," the girl said with a brief, curious glance. "I'll take over here." And she reached for the pitchfork.

Wren raced upstairs to the wing she had learned was used exclusively by the Browns' leaders and other toffs. On the way she met Connor, who was being led by a messenger. Connor's face wore that expression of polite blankness she'd seen him use when she'd glimpsed him among his relations at court functions.

Wondering if they were in trouble, she fell in step beside him.

They were shown into a room high in the biggest tower. Its windows afforded a spectacular view of the entire valley. Before the windows stood a short, stocky man with a pointed gray beard. He was dressed exactly like the rest of the Browns, without any special insignia marking his rank.

As soon as the door closed, he said, "Sit down, you two."

They dropped onto two chairs waiting before a wide desk.

The Commander studied them for a moment from dark eyes under bushy brows. "Wren and . . . Falstan. Do I have that right?"

Connor said nothing, giving only the briefest of nods, so Wren spoke firmly: "You do."

"We questioned one of the persons we apprehended at the time we found you, and he told us some strange stories. One of which is that the son of Duke Fortian of Meldrith sent them to arrest you." The Commander smiled frostily. "Unfortunately, they were not able to exhibit for us the writ of criminal pursuit that we require of anyone conducting that sort of business in Siradayel. Do you know anything about this?"

"It's true that some of Duke Fortian's messengers have been chasing us," Wren said, not hiding her indignation, "but we don't know why. We're not criminals. You can send a message to the Magic School in Cantirmoor about me—about both of us—and they'll tell you that."

102

"Unfortunately we do not have a magician among our ranks," the Commander said.

"Well, I could try to scry them for you," Wren offered. "Even though I'm not supposed to yet—"

He waved her to silence. "If you were the criminals your pursuers named you, you could easily set up someone to appear in your magic glass and claim to be the King of Meldrith, and we wouldn't know if it was truth or illusion. You indicated your business with us was a search of the records?"

"It is," Wren said. "That's all, and why anyone wants to chase us—" She stopped, sliding a hasty look at Connor, who sat up straight, his expression troubled.

"Was this the information you sought?"

The Commander pulled a yellowed paper off his desk and held it out to Wren, who snatched at it eagerly, her eyes scanning the neatly written report. Words leapt out at her, their sense barely clear:

> . . . *caravan . . . dead . . . Alive were one boy and one girl. . . . The girl is aged between one and two, has brown hair, blue eyes, was wearing a green garment after the fashion of Allat Los's valley cities. Word has been dispatched to Kiel. The child will be held one season pending message from any kin registered there.*

Wren looked up to find the Commander watching her, his expression not unkind.

"This is it," she said, feeling as if the ground were dissolving beneath her feet. *Green garment . . . Allat Los . . . That's really me.* Her head buzzed.

"You may copy what you like from it at this desk here; we do not permit these records to go out of this area. Master Falstan, you may come with me," the Commander said to Connor. Though distracted, Wren thought his tone was oddly formal for addressing a journeyman player. "I understand you were ill when you arrived. I will conduct you on a little

103

tour of our fortress." The Commander gestured toward the door.

Wren turned to the desk and dipped a pen.

At that moment, back in Cantirmoor's royal palace, Teressa ran up the marble stairs in the royal wing, shaking raindrops from her hair.

It had almost been a relief when the sudden rain squall spoiled her first party. She had invited the daughter of the new ambassador from Eth Lamrec for a ride, along with several other girls she did not know well, all of whom were from northern marches. To her surprise, all had accepted her invitation.

The idea had been to work on her Lamreci, *which seemed a good idea in the middle of the night, but wasn't so great in practice,* she thought ruefully. Remembering the stilted, painstaking conversation and her own frequent grammatical mistakes, she decided it was time to study her languages a little harder.

When she reached the hallway outside her parents' suite, a short woman walked out of the sitting room and stopped when she saw Teressa.

"Aunt Leila!"

"I was just coming to look for you. How did your riding party go?" the magician asked as they went into the sitting room, where Queen Astren was waiting.

Teressa shook her head. "Not too well, I'm afraid." She gave a brief explanation.

"You're too hard on yourself," her mother said, laying down her pen. "That was very well done. You don't seem to realize how flattered the ambassador was when you singled out her daughter like that."

"But the dull conversation—" Teressa protested.

"The thing was, you tried to speak *her* language, rather than make her speak yours. Her Siradi isn't very good yet, either, you must have noticed," Aunt Leila said.

Teressa laughed. "Somehow, when people are trying to speak my language, I think their mistakes are fun, and I don't mind. But I was embarrassed at the way I mangled hers."

"Did she seem angry?" the Queen asked.

Teressa shook her head.

"Then she probably feels the same way you do," Aunt Leila said briskly, an impish smile on her usually severe face. "Now. We have a little intrigue for you."

"My dear, your aunt Carlas wants to see you," the Queen said. "Right now. In the Emerald Room."

Teressa wrinkled her nose. "Aunt Carlas?"

Aunt Leila and the Queen exchanged looks, both of them on the verge of laughing. "Our good cousin Carlas has a late birthday present for you, something supposedly arranged by your father after your most strenuous request," Leila said. "Your father graciously allowed her to assume the heavy cost of the gift, which is why she is giving it to you."

"What?" Teressa asked, confused. "I never asked for anything. Oh! Is this some kind of hoax?"

"Yes, but one *we* arranged, most carefully. Our dear Duchess Carlas, being her usual sweet self, is now acting as if it were her own idea—which I'm telling you now so that you won't refuse her gift," Leila added.

"I'll tell you more as we walk downstairs, my dear," the Queen murmured. "And I regret the necessity of the hoax, but we must find out who is behind the vexing things happening in court."

"And I'm to help?" Teressa asked.

Her mother and aunt both nodded. Teressa looked from one to the other, realizing that they were *trusting* her, that they were treating her like one of themselves.

"I must leave you now," Leila put in, moving toward the door, "because I—as a mere magician—was not invited to attend Carlas's presentation. You will be *so* surprised and delighted, I must warn you. Do you think you can manage that?"

"No matter what it is," Teressa said with conviction, "if

105

it means I'm fooling Aunt Carlas, I can be just as delighted as you like."

Laughing together, the three of them left the room.

Connor followed along, looking to the left or right at whatever the Commander indicated. The man kept up a commentary on the functions of the various parts of the fortress, scarcely pausing for Connor to reply. Not that Connor wanted to talk; he was afraid that the Commander had somehow found out who he really was.

When they reached the high northern wall the Commander stopped. A cold wind buffeted Connor's face as he stared out at the mountains dropping away toward the plains of Siradayel, the country his mother ruled. He clasped his hands tightly behind him and said nothing.

For a time the Commander looked out over the land in silence, then he turned to face Connor. "I would like a true answer to one question, and then you may answer subsequent questions as your conscience permits."

Connor's heart banged against his ribs. "Very well," he said, glad his voice sounded even.

The Commander gave a short nod. "Did the two of you in fact depart from Cantirmoor with the permission of your guardians, or did you . . . choose to depart on your own?"

Connor could answer that one. Trying to hide his relief, he said steadily, "The magicians permitted Wren to make this journey. They know all about her quest. And they asked me to accompany her."

The Commander's gaze was uncomfortably direct, but Connor met it squarely.

Another short nod, and the Commander said, "Then that's that." He turned to look out over the land again and added, "We don't always hear much about other countries, isolated as we are, but word of troubles in Cantirmoor has reached even us. And we've seen evidence of troubles closer by."

Remembering their journey through the forest, Connor felt a flush of anger. He knew his face was turning red, but he couldn't stop it. "Brigands," he said when the Commander looked at him questioningly. "Forest is full of them. And those fellows yesterday were not Blues. They were probably hired brigands."

"Probably." The Commander pursed his lips. "Our lordly neighbors seem to be busy elsewhere and don't patrol their woodlands much. Travelers have been complaining to us of frequent robberies. You'd increase the patrols, then?"

Connor thought for a moment, then burst out, "It's a sign of bad provincial government. Not *all* those people could have chosen brigandage over any other way to make a living. Too many of them means—" Connor suddenly remembered that most ordinary boys knew nothing about governing provinces—and cared less.

The Commander appeared to notice nothing amiss. He continued Connor's thought. "When the overlord is always absent, the local barons are left unsupervised. Some follow their lord to the capital, leaving the land effectively ungoverned, and some feel free to institute rules of their own. Heavier taxes, say. So that some folk who cannot pay are forced out of their homes, and those homes are filled with people obedient to the new laws."

Connor's hands gripped even more tightly behind him, but he said nothing. If he were King Verne, he would have called Fortian and his precious barons to account long ago.

But he wasn't. He was Connor, Prince of Siradayel— landless and worthless in everyone's eyes. Everyone's except, perhaps, his few friends'.

The silence stretched as the Commander waited for him to return an answer. Then the man shrugged and turned his back on the view. "We learn by observation," he said. "And it never hurts to observe, and learn, as much as we can, even when we cannot act directly. One never knows what the future might bring." He started walking toward the stairs.

"Do you think you and your companion will want to journey into Allat Los?"

Connor thought of Wren and the look on her face when she read the paper the Commander had given her. "If we can."

The Commander's weathered face creased with distinct humor. "She has worked hard down in our stable, and I think the week we'd assigned her as payment can be cut short. As it happens, we have a patrol going along the northern border tomorrow morning at dawn. They sometimes permit travelers to ride with them, if they can keep pace."

"We won't slow them," Connor said. "Thank you."

"Part of our duties," the Commander said. "Thank the Queen"—he smiled wryly—"should you happen to meet her."

Chapter Eleven

"... and here is your present, my *dear* child." Carlas bestowed a gracious smile on Teressa, indicating the ruddy-haired dog sitting behind her. The little group of courtiers, most of them Carlas's most devoted followers, clapped and *oooooh*'d.

Teressa looked at the long, lean hound with the bushy brown fur and the foxlike ears and muzzle. The dog looked back at her, and his tail stirred.

"You'll enjoy having a true friend," Carlas went on in her sweetest voice.

Hinting that I can't make friends with people, Teressa thought. But she knew she could make friends—she'd been proving that lately. *Which is probably why Carlas had to say it,* she realized. She felt a sudden urge to laugh, and she turned the impulse into a big smile of gratitude.

"You are so *kind,* Aunt Carlas," she said.

"Go ahead, call him," Carlas said, so pleased she sounded almost human. "He is very well trained—a highly bred animal, I assure you."

Teressa looked at the dog, hesitating. He cocked his ears and panted gently.

"Go on," Mirlee said to the dog in a sharp voice. "Go!"

The dog just sat, looking up at Teressa. Mirlee gave him a push, but he went forward only a step, then lay down, head cocked. Some people tittered.

Teressa clapped lightly. "Come," and she held out her hand.

"He's stupid—" Mirlee sneered.

The dog trotted forward and sat at Teressa's feet.

"Up." She snapped her fingers.

The hound stood on his hind legs, dancing forward a step or two. The people watching laughed and exclaimed.

"Speak!" Teressa said.

The dog gave a bark, ears flopping.

Teressa turned to her aunt. "He's wonderful. We'll have such fun—thank you." She pulled the green velvet ribbon from her hair and tied it around the dog's neck.

Several of the watchers began to crowd around, everyone wanting to pet the princess's new hound, who wagged his tail. Behind them, Teressa overhead Garian say to his sister, "Stupid, huh! He just won't listen to *you*."

"He's ugly, anyway," Mirlee retorted sulkily. "I'll get myself a prettier one."

Then their conversation was drowned out by the exclamations of others, all of whom wanted a handsome, well-trained dog *today*.

"Come, we'll get you some water," Teressa said, moving toward the door. The hound trotted obediently at her heels, causing a fresh outburst of compliments.

When they were safely outside, Teressa gave in to her laughter. Then, looking down at the shaggy head next to her, she said, "I think, Tyron, you're going to be very, very popular."

Two days later, high in the mountains of Siradayel, the leader of the Brown patrol stopped his pony and pointed down through the mist-shrouded valleys into Allat Los. "There lies your path," he said.

Wren felt her heart start galloping.

She'd thoroughly enjoyed the two-day ride through the mountains, though she'd found herself hoping something awful would happen, just so the Browns could get rid of whoever was chasing them.

Maybe our pursuers have given up, Wren thought. *I'm glad Mistress Leila didn't make us stay in Pelsir.* Still, she felt a twinge of guilt.

Right after Connor had told her of the Commander's offer, she'd gone straight to her room to get out her scry-stone. Even though she was afraid the malevolent sorcerer might be listening in, she'd risked contacting the school—and had been relieved when she got Mistress Leila.

Wren had been able to sense how reluctant the school authorities were to let her continue her quest, but they had given in when she promised that she and Connor would have an escort of Browns. What she had not told Mistress Leila was that the escort would last only as long as her quest and their regular path lay along the same road. *We're probably safe,* she thought, banishing the guilt. *Surely if anyone were going to pounce, it would have happened right when we left Pelsir.*

Wren felt a tug of regret that they'd be leaving the Browns, who knew lots of good stories and songs to tell around the campfire at night. But they were border patrollers, and Wren's quest now led down into Allat Los.

One more stop, and either she lost the trail forever—or she found her goal. Every time she thought about how close she might be to the end of her quest, her heart seemed to squeeze inside her. She'd memorized those words on the paper the Commander had shown her, *The child will be held one season pending a message from kin . . .* She knew what that meant: Either she'd had no kin registered in Kiel, in which case she was still an orphan and her trail was cold, or else she *did* have kin but they had not come to get her. She couldn't decide which would be worse.

She dismounted from her pony and gave him a final pat. He *whuff*-ed against her cheek, shifting as she unlashed her pack.

Hefting his own pack, Connor walked a little way along

the path, then turned to wait. He'd been very quiet during the two-day ride, leaving Wren to carry on their share of general conversation.

"Many thanks," Wren said, smiling up at the patrol leader.

He saluted. "Have a safe trip." He clucked to his pony.

Both Wren and Connor watched as the patrol disappeared around the side of a cliff. Then Connor surprised Wren by letting out a long sigh.

"You think they guessed who you are?"

"I *know* they guessed." Connor grimaced. "But as near as I can figure, the fact that no one said anything means that, officially at least, they don't have to do anything about us. The Commander did ask me if we were runaways."

"After all I told them!" Wren exclaimed. "Didn't they believe me?"

"Supposedly a prince doesn't lie." Connor gave a sour smile. "Obviously they've never met some of my family." He shook his head. "Enough of that. Your paper didn't say much. How did they know that Kiel is the city where you'll find your answer?"

Wren slid her hand into her tunic, touching the paper she'd copied from the Browns' records. "The record keeper told me. They identified the caravan by the goods it had been carrying. Nearly everything it carried could have come from almost anywhere—cloth, mostly, and some embroidered silk flowers, which were popular among the toffs back then—but there was also a certain kind of rice paper. Real thin and smooth, and it lasts for centuries, the record keeper told me. And it only comes from one place, and they only sell a certain amount a year, which keeps the price high."

"So you'll be able to go to the tax collector in Kiel, have them look up a caravan that paid export tax on rice paper for the year thirty-one twenty-one—"

"Five hundred fourteen, if they don't use Council reckoning," Wren put in.

"They've got to, if they're traders. It's the traders who

keep the Council years," Connor said. "Much easier for record keeping than having to know it's five-fourteen in Allat Los—"

"Which is the same as eight hundred sixty-four, Rhis time," Wren said. "Isn't it strange, all the ways we count years? Anyway, then I find out who was registered to that caravan, if they had a baby around two years old . . . and who might be listed as kin." *And if kin are listed, find out why they didn't come.*

She broke off when a shadow crossed the sun. Just for a moment, but it was enough to make them both whirl around. Wren saw a long black speck moving rapidly away from the sun.

Connor's face paled. "Another spybird. Its mind was blanked. I couldn't hear it."

"Let's hide—"

"Too late. It saw us, all right. We'd better get away from here."

Wren pointed across the windswept mountain slopes. "See—just beyond there? A lake! It must be Arath Ir, and there's got to be lots of greenery around there to hide in."

As soon as she spoke, Wren thought of the forest fire, and she could tell by the way Connor's lips tightened that he was thinking of it, too. But he said nothing, just started to run. Wren started after, muttering the words of the protection spell. She closed her mind for a second, imagining it firmly in place over them both—and when she released, the spell held. *That'll keep us safe for a time*, she thought, *though it won't help the countryside. Who is chasing us? Why?*

As they ran, one or other of them kept looking back, and finally Wren spotted a line of riders way up the mountainside, on the same trail they'd been taking. She stopped, and Connor, seeing her, stopped, too.

"Wren? We can't stay here. We've got to hurry," Connor gasped.

She just shook her head, saving her breath for her spell. Facing back up the trail, she pulled out her magic book. With trembling fingers, she paged through in search of a shift spell. Finding it, she glanced through the carefully noted variations for different kind of objects, then, muttering the words, she fixed her gaze on a huge boulder resting just beside the narrow trail.

The spell pulled oddly at her, so she stopped and began again, putting all her focus into it. Slowly her hands came together, and suddenly the cliffside beside the trail exploded, stones flying in all directions.

Wren and Connor ducked a rain of dirt clods, and Connor whistled. "That will certainly take care of anyone who wants to come down this way."

"I only meant to shift the one boulder," Wren said numbly, the backwash from the powerful magic making her momentarily dizzy. "I muffed it somehow, and all the stones moved. I'm not supposed to be doing this . . ."

"Illusions aren't going to help us now."

"True, but if any creatures had been about . . ." Wren breathed slowly, forcing the dizziness away. "I can see why Tyron said beginners who experiment recklessly are more dangerous than most evil magicians"—she drew another shaky breath—"though I thought it a fairly low insult at the time!"

"I think we ought to hurry along," Connor said.

"I'm ready."

Once again they began to run.

While Wren and Connor ran down the mountainside toward the lake, back in Cantirmoor Teressa walked into her mother's inner chamber, grabbed up a goblet she saw on a side table, and poured water into it.

"Thirsty work, daughter?" the Queen asked.

Teressa nodded, draining the cup.

"Talking?" Leila asked from the other side of the room.

"Not talking," Teressa said. "*Listening*. I think I have spent time with every single person in the entire court, and all of them want to talk my ear off if given half a chance."

The Queen patted the couch next to her and Teressa dropped down gratefully. As Astren's silken arm came around her, Teressa leaned against her mother and looked around in contentment. This inner chamber was her favorite in the palace, a comfortable one with plain furniture that you could really rest on, and only one piece of artwork: a tapestry of children dancing.

"Is our plot working?" the Queen asked. "From my vantage, things seem exactly the same as ever. Two quarrels this morning, one over a valuable manuscript stolen during the night."

"We don't really know yet," Leila said, turning to Teressa. "I take it you have heard nothing out of the ordinary?"

"Talk, talk, and more talk," Teressa said. "Some of it was fun, and some was dull, but none of it was of any importance."

"Where's Tyron?" Leila asked, quick concern in her eyes.

"Making his report in to Halfrid," Teressa said, and her aunt relaxed a little.

Queen Astren rose from the couch to stand at the window, looking down at the fountain in the courtyard. She seemed worried. Teressa fought against a yawn; she had stayed up very late at a party given by Perd's mother, but the boys had not disappeared, nor had they sneaked off for a private talk.

The Queen turned to look at her sister. "What kind of report does he make if he cannot talk? How will we know if this plan is working?"

"His 'reporting in' is for us to check on his well-being," Leila said reassuringly. "The moment he hears something of importance he will come straight to us. And as soon as he has his natural shape back he will tell us everything."

Queen Astren sighed. "It is dangerous, his being a dog, isn't it? I must say, I mislike it more as each day goes by."

"It's not easy, shape-shifting," Leila said. "But he knew that. This is why we check him every day. He'll stay in his dog shape for a short time longer, and if he still has discovered nothing, we'll quietly return him to his own shape and substitute a real dog in his place. Meanwhile, he's been welcomed by everyone all over the palace—Carlas and her family dote on him, just as we'd expected."

"Even Mirlee," Teressa said with a laugh. "He does just what she asks him, now."

Teressa saw her mother's lips twitch. "It was a good idea, talking them into giving that 'present.' "

"Oh, Carlas claims it was her idea."

"She paid well enough to say anything she likes," the Queen replied. "I felt bad, asking so large a sum for what is essentially a trick."

Aunt Leila laughed. "Don't. It was the only way to guarantee they'd believe it. They only value what is costly, our Rhismordith cousins." Aunt Leila turned to face Teressa. "How do you feel about our trickery?"

"Well, they all like him. The shape he took is a rare breed from somewhere very exotic, I gather, and Garian and his friends just love it when he comes with me to parties. I've started a fashion! Now everyone wants a dog. Mirlee is mad about that," Teressa added. "None of Garian's dogs will pay her the least mind."

"It is unsettling to Carlas and her daughter to see you suddenly in a position of leadership among the young people," the Queen said.

"Which is where you belong," Leila put in, with a good deal of satisfaction. "But you had better watch out for them. If I know Carlas, she'll be teaching that girl ways to make you look foolish, if she can."

"I'm twice as polite to Mirlee as to anyone else," Teressa said. "Whenever I see her, I give her a smile as big as the sun. I think she's more confused right now than anything else."

"Good," Leila said. "We don't need any more trouble than we already have—"

"One thing I've noticed, my child," said a new voice at

the door, "I've never seen a happier dog. I think your magician likes his new shape."

Teressa turned. "Papa!" she cried happily. It was seldom she got to see her parents together without hordes of servants or courtiers about.

The King dropped a kiss on Teressa's head before moving to the window to stand next to his wife.

Teressa smiled up at her father, but she felt troubled at the phrase *your magician*. She knew what it meant. Tyron, as Halfrid's heir, would someday be King's Magician—or if the King was right, Queen's Magician.

She looked at her father. His dark, neatly trimmed beard and his thick hair showed just a little sprinkling of gray. His eyes were alert, and he was still as fit as any of his Scarlet Guard. Teressa hated even the thought of losing him. Or her mother. *I've gotten accustomed to being a princess*, she thought. *But I hope I will never have to be Queen.*

"I, too, have noticed Tyron having fun," Leila said. "Teressa, his visit to Halfrid must be over by now. Maybe you should go check on your pet, see what he's gotten into. Don't let him adopt any nasty doggy habits."

The adults all laughed, and Teressa smiled back at them before she left.

"They're gaining!" Wren cried, her breath ragged.

"Take the shortcut." Connor pointed across a long, rocky meadow to some cliffs.

Beyond the promontory the world seemed to end. They'd seen the cliffs from another angle, and Connor knew that they afforded only a long drop into the water.

Wren's cheeks paled and she shivered.

"Can you swim?" Connor asked.

"Well, yes, but it's not often . . . I've had to swim in water . . . deeper than I could walk in . . ."

"Better that than them, right?" He pointed over his shoulder at the distant line of dust.

Wren's mouth tightened. "All right. I'll see if I can manage to put our packs . . . in a protection that seals them."

As they ran, Wren fumbled with her book, nearly stumbling several times. Connor divided his attention between watching the pursuers and warning Wren away from the biggest obstacles in her path.

When they reached the cliffs, they stopped and dropped their packs, breathing hard. Connor sat down and yanked off his boots, thrusting them into his pack. Then he gazed down at the lake water gleaming and winking far below. He felt his stomach drop, as if he'd already jumped without knowing it. Still, it was better to do something than to stand still and wait to be caught. He doubted if the pursuers would jump in after them. And if they did, at least they'd be no faster in the water than Wren and Connor.

"There! Can you touch it? Not the strap, the bag." Wren pointed.

Connor put his hand down, feeling a strange interference between his fingers and his worn knapsack. This gave him an idea. "Can you put this bubble around us? So we can breathe underwater?"

"I was going to try, but what if we used up all the air in it?"

"Right."

Connor noticed that the chasers were suddenly much closer. So close, in fact, he could see the leader hefting some kind of weapon—

"Let's go," he urged.

Wren's shoulders hunched. "I—"

"Just follow me, and don't think about it. We'll be all right, if we go *now*."

Connor threw his pack and his staff over, then dove after them.

The trip through the air seemed long. And—it was strange, how magic glimmered unseen in the air around him. It felt as if he had only to stretch out his arms and he'd soar over the water . . .

The air around him seemed to slow, as if he were riding an air current. He flung his arms wide, almost seeing them take the shape of feathered wings—and then he was startled by a dark shape plummeting past him.

He lost the thought, and his equilibrium, too, falling to splash hard in the water. His nose and mouth filled with water, and he fought his way to the surface, gasping and coughing.

Wren bobbed a short distance away, her eyes wide under her streaming brown hair. "How did you *do* that? Stay in the air like that?" she yelled.

"Do what?"

Splash!

A spear landed just an arm's length from Connor.

"Dive down! Fast!" Wren yelled.

Another and another hit the water around them, murderously close.

Connor sucked in a deep breath and dove down, swimming away as fast as his heavy clothing would permit.

Thousands of bubbles rose in his face, making vision difficult. He swam until he thought his lungs would catch fire, then he came up for air. Almost immediately a huge rock splashed into the water nearby, pitching a wave of cold water into his face. He heard Wren give a cry of fear, but he couldn't get the water from his eyes.

Come, Skylord, a voice urged.

What?

His mouth opened—and cold water flowed in. He choked, clawing for the surface.

Take our shape, then you can breathe—

The voice spoke inside his head, louder now, and insistent.

He broke surface, gasped air in, and dove. His clothes seemed to weigh as much as one of those boulders, and he knew he couldn't keep swimming like this much longer.

Come, hear me. Take our shape. The voice was next to him—inside him.

119

Suddenly he saw his arms spreading, shaping . . .

Over that came the terrifying memory of the lightning he caused, up on the mountain, when the forest fire threatened to destroy them; and the vision splintered—

Again! You almost had it.

And again he saw his hands glowing with blue, taking magic from the air and water in faint ribbons of light—

Touch your companion, give her the shape.

Lightning flashed, stung him from head to heels. He threw the lightning toward Wren—

Then he drew a deep breath and watched bubbles stream harmlessly away from him, out of his gills.

Chapter Twelve

*W*ren sucked in a deep breath and watched the bubbles stream from the sides of her face toward the surface. Her vision was suddenly clear. She studied her hands, which were covered slickly by a greenish silver skin. Webbing stretched between her fingers.

A yell of joy escaped her, the sound coming out a blur. She laughed and watched the laughter escape in a froth of bubbles toward the surface.

She turned to look for Connor. A strange figure waved its limbs nearby. Its head was vaguely human, except that it had no nose; a finlike membrane went from its scalp down its back. She knew it was Connor only by his clothes, which billowed ridiculously in the water. Otherwise he was so different she had to laugh again—this time in wonder.

Once more, blue-white shiny bubbles rose from her mouth, blocking her vision. When they disappeared, she saw Connor struggling to pull off his tunic and shirt, spinning slowly in the water as he tugged and yanked. Becoming aware of her own heavy brown magician's garb dragging at her, she fought the sash loose with her webbed hands, then dove out of her clothes. Wadding them into a ball, she tied them with the sash.

Then, looking in delight down her fish-smooth body, she experimented with turning and diving in the water. Her legs felt different, longer and less bony. Her feet were webbed at the toes. *Frog legs,* she thought.

Bringing her fingers to her face, she felt her nose, a smooth, flat bump, with long nostrils. She felt them widen to let the cool water rush in, then close again as bubbles streamed out the gills beside her ears.

Looking for Connor again, she was startled not to recognize him immediately. He was surrounded by a number of fish-people, and without his human clothes he looked just like them. Swimming closer, she spotted him by the bubble-surrounded pack he held by its strap.

Wren found her own pack suspended in the water a short distance away, and she snagged it. Connor beckoned to her just then, and she launched herself toward him, noticing how powerfully her new legs propelled her through the water. How had he done that magic? She'd heard nothing—felt nothing—until a hand grabbed her and a flash of light blinded her.

Connor gestured again, and the fish-people flowed around him, moving swiftly and gracefully downward. Wren glanced up and saw blue sky beyond the glistening surface. Here and there a huge rock smashed down, sinking fast, but Wren counted fewer than before.

They must think we've drowned, Wren thought in satisfaction. *Maybe we are rid of them at last.*

But what next? Where are we going?

Even with her clear underwater sight, she could not see very far. The lake water was a deep blue in the distance, broken occasionally by slanting rays of sunlight.

Down and down they swam, until they brushed against the tops of waving green fronds. Still downward, until tall, uneven shadows resolved slowly into rocks. Down through a huge opening, into darkness—then sudden light illuminated round rock tunnels. Glow-globes at intervals marked out the tunnels through the striated rock. The water was cool and still.

There were fish-people of all sizes, some of them with

long pale hair streaming out, others with fin membranes like hers. Wren noticed in the light of the globes that their bodies had subtle patterns of colors, mostly greens, blues, and silver. By these patterns she would have to tell them apart; the strange faces, partly human and partly not, all looked the same. Between the people, different kinds of fish either darted or glided.

On and on they swam, until Wren realized they were now over a kind of city built into the rock. At last they dove down into a cavernous room with glow-globes set into the walls. Connor and those leading him came to rest on a shelf of jutting rock.

Wren saw Connor's head bent in concentration. A small fish-person sat nearby, looking intently into his face. Larger ones crowded around, all poised motionless in the water except for tiny movements when the currents shifted, all facing Connor.

It was obvious they were communicating. Wren thought about the way Connor "heard" animals, and she guessed this worked much the same way. It was also obvious that she wasn't going to have any part of it.

So she set her pack-bubble under a stone shelf, where it bobbed gently, trying to rise toward the surface. Moving a little way off, she experimented with swimming. It was as close to flying as she would ever come. She tried somersaults and dives, and each time her speed increased. It was so much fun that she was startled when a fish-person appeared next to her and touched her arm. A voice said somewhere inside her head, *Come.*

She saw Connor beckon to her. She gave two smooth kicks and reached him. He grasped her wrist, and she heard his voice inside her head: *They don't know much Siradi, and I guess you can't hear anyone except when you are touching, am I right?*

Wren opened her mouth, saw bubbles, nodded instead.

We are safe here. These people are telling me lots of new things. We'll stay with them tonight, but tomorrow they'll take us to the other side of the lake, which means we'll be right above Kiel. Along with the words came a wash of emotions, a sense of longing and regret. Connor really wanted to stay, but there was some reason why he couldn't.

Wren carefully said inside her head, *Are they worried about those toadwarts who were chasing us?*

No—at least, I don't think so. There is some reason why we must return to Cantirmoor, though.

Is someone in Cantirmoor in danger—or is it us?

Connor's thought came back, confused and worried. *I don't know. They use more images than words, and they go so fast. And what words they do use don't always make sense. But maybe I'll learn more before tomorrow.*

Will you tell me what you learn?

I will.

Connor let go of her, and a new swarm of fish-people came up carrying containers full of food. It was cold and chewy and green, but Wren was hungry.

After they ate, the smaller fish-people crowded around her. Wren copied their gestures, which turned into a game. Soon she was playing a kind of complicated tag with them; it involved lots of fast swimming around and through rocky structures. Wren loved it, playing hard until she realized quite suddenly that she was tired.

When she looked about, she noticed some of the fish-people lying gently on rock shelves. Swimming closer, she saw that they were asleep. Since no one seemed to care what she did, she stretched out near some of the people her own size and closed her eyes, rocked gently by tiny ripples in the still, cool water.

"Tyron!"

Tyron scrambled to a stop and looked back at Teressa. The cold early-morning wind ruffled through his fur, bringing interesting scents to tease his nose. He whined softly, wanting to run with the other dogs. What did she want, anyway?

He looked back and saw her pounding determinedly after him, her skirts bunched in her hands. Before his shape-change he had never appreciated just how slow and clumsy human bodies were.

Teressa caught up, breathing hard. "Why did you run off like that? You're the only one who can listen to Garian and Nyl and the others, and they're talking back there on the terrace."

Talking about nothing interesting, Tyron thought. *Just sitting around. And the wind beckons* . . . Still, he knew he had a job to do.

As yet he had not found the evidence they were seeking. Every time he listened to Garian, he just heard more of the usual bragging or arguing, and Marit and Perd were not much better. The fourth member of their group, Hawk the foreigner, seldom talked at all.

So Tyron had begun avoiding them, far more interested in the fun he was having as a dog than in the affairs of people. *Their voices sound as shrill as birds when they jabber*, he thought morosely; sharp, high voices irritated him.

Then he shook his head. *I've been a dog too long*, he thought. *It's getting harder to return to my human thoughts.*

Just then a howl caught his attention. It was a loud, challenging howl, coming from the direction of the King's Park. With it came a cacophony of excited barks from the other palace dogs.

Tyron's steps lagged. He knew what that howl meant. It was a challenge from . . . a new dog. Tyron was leader of all the palace dogs. They all sensed that he was something special, and they had deferred to him, following him on long, fun chases.

But a new dog had appeared just today, a silvery wolfhound. Tyron had been seeking him when Teressa called.

"Oooo-ooooowww!" the howl came again.

The triumph in that voice made Tyron's fur prickle.

There's something . . . something strange . . .

He turned and raced off, nose to the ground, tracking

the scent of the pack. He picked up their trail just as another howl sounded. They were running east now.

Shortcut. Tyron plunged through the underbrush, scarcely hearing Teressa's shouts behind him.

Streaking over streams and through tall grasses, Tyron raced, rejoicing in his speed. Another shortcut and he'd close in on their new leader, who seemed to be making a circuit of the great park.

He caught sight of a flash of silver fur ahead as the wolfhound's long shape soared over a low stone wall. Putting on a burst of speed, Tyron caught up. The other dog showed teeth, stretching its legs in a harder run. Tyron was inches shorter, but that did not matter: here was a challenge to his leadership. He *had* to win.

The two of them raced on, leaving the other dogs behind. When at last the wolfhound slowed, Tyron growled, prepared for battle—but a human voice caught at his awareness, and an old feeling, one he'd nearly forgotten, singed his nerves: *magic.*

"So here's our foxy friend," whispered the voice. "Let's just see what you might be hiding." Danger emanated from that voice.

And before Tyron could turn and leap for the speaker's throat, a white light blinded him and he fell, stunned, to the grass.

"Oh," Wren groaned. "I'm heavy."

"No, you're normal," Connor said with a laugh as he came out from behind a shrub, dressed in his spare clothes. He reached up to tie his dripping hair back with a narrow black ribbon.

Wren smoothed her second tunic down and bent to pick up her old tunic. She wrung it out, watching lake water splash onto the dirt. "I *feel* heavy. And so does this."

"If we put our old clothes into our packs they'll spoil

everything," Connor said. "Why not hang them over our packs to dry in the sun?"

Wren nodded, and they helped each other arrange their garments, then they set out on the narrow pathway. Connor walked in silence, his face preoccupied.

After a short time, Wren said, "Well?"

Startled, Connor blinked at her. "Well, what?"

Wren said, "I've been patient. I've been good, *and* quiet, but if you don't tell me just what happened back there in that lake, then you are going to learn what happens when I lose my temper!"

"I'll try," he said. "But I don't know everything—how could I? Only three of them knew any Siradi, and they tend to give information by sharing memories. I didn't always understand what I was seeing."

"Sharing memories? How?"

Connor looked at the ground before he spoke. "As you discovered, they talk mind to mind," he said at last. "Without sound. They have a kind of language, but mostly they use images. And they keep records by sharing memories. I saw a lot, and some of it I suspect is from hundreds of years ago, but there's no way to tell, for they don't measure time in years."

"Did you find out more about that danger in Cantirmoor?"

"No," Connor said, frowning at the trail. "They seemed to think they had said enough, or that I'd understood more than I had. Usually they don't have much to do with humans, and I'm not sure that they would have interfered if we'd just been a couple of regular folk."

"They knew you are a prince?"

Connor gave his head a quick shake. "No. That kind of thing doesn't mean anything to them. They knew—and they didn't tell me *how* they knew—that I've got Iyon Daiyin ancestors."

Wren whistled. "You told us that once. When you told

us about your talent." She added tentatively, "You didn't seem to want to talk about it, then, and we didn't ask. But now . . ."

"Well, I don't know a lot more. My father told me some things before he died, but I was barely five, and I didn't understand much of it." He frowned. "Though some of it seems to be coming back," he said in a low voice, so low Wren almost missed it.

Wren felt questions burning in her mind, but she could tell from Connor's thoughtful, slightly disturbed expression that he was not finding any of this easy.

"I know a little more now, but the more I find out, the more mysterious it all seems. The Iyon Daiyin were folk from another world. *Daiyin* was the name of the world, and *iyon* was their word for 'people.' Actually, it was more like 'People Running Away From.' "

"Another *world*," Wren murmured, feeling that surge of intense longing to travel not just around this world but to others.

"And they had lots of magic, which diminished in time as they mixed with people here and had children. For some reason the mountain peaks make the talents stronger. Either that, or there's more magic up here . . ." He paused, looking around through distant-seeing eyes. "That explains what I've sensed every time I travel in mountains . . ."

Wren bit down on her lip, wanting to shout, *What? How? Why?*

Connor shook his head. "But whatever it is, I'm losing it. I can feel it going, each step we take away from the heights."

"I take it you won't be able to douse fires when we get to low land," Wren said carefully.

"I don't know how much of that I can do anyway," Connor said quickly. "This is one thing the fish-folk impressed on me. They called me *Skylord*, which was their name for the Iyon Daiyin. It was because the Iyon Daiyin used to shape-change and fly as birds. Some of them also had talents, and one of those was the ability to manage winds and weather." He gave a rueful shrug. "I seem to have inherited that one, too. But it's dangerous. Causing storms like the one I raised to douse the fire *can* do more harm than good. So I guess I have a talent I can only use in mountains, and then I *shouldn't* use it."

"Did they tell you much about themselves?"

"Not much," he said. "They are very shy of humans. I don't know how they even knew we were coming, but they did. Their magic is a different kind from either mine or yours. Yet they want me to come back, because they have much to teach me . . ." He turned suddenly, looking back up the trail toward the lake. "And I do want to go! But we have to finish the business at hand first."

"I'd like to go with you if you do," Wren said.

Connor laughed. "Somehow I knew that was coming. They called you Tadpole-Will-Jump-Streams, and I got the feeling that you'd be welcome."

"Tadpole-Will-Jump-Streams? What does that mean?"

Connor paused on the cliff, looking down. Below lay the city of Kiel, spread out in the shape of a great wheel.

Wren waited for his answer, staring at the streets and the tiny houses and the occasional glint of the sun on metal or glass. For a moment the city seemed closed in, bound to the dirt. Her vantage lent her distance, but only until she remembered, with a strong heart tug, her errand there.

Connor spoke again. "I have a feeling it means that you, too, have talents of a different kind. But you haven't found them yet."

Chapter Thirteen

*O*h, there you are, you naughty dog!" Teressa exclaimed, trying to hide her relief.

Aunt Carlas sniffed with ladylike disapproval. "He seems to have run through a mud pile."

Teressa held out her hand, and the ruddy-colored hound jumped up on the terrace beside Teressa, sniffed her fingers, then dropped beside her, tongue lolling, the green velvet ribbon round his neck speckled with dots of mud.

Aunt Carlas turned away, and in a honey-sweet voice began to tell the Queen and the other ladies just what had been wrong with a party given the night before by a lady who was not now present.

Teressa sat a little behind the adults, in a circle of girls more or less her own age. The girls were gossiping idly, and Teressa knew she ought to be listening in case someone let fall a scrap of information that might be helpful to her parents. However, she was tired from so many late nights in a row, and for a moment or two it was nice just to sit back in the gentle sunlight and let her eyes wander over the fresh blooms in the garden.

"Don't *you* think so, Cousin Teressa?"

Teressa's thought splintered at the sound of her cousin Mirlee's sharp voice. She turned, schooling her face into polite inquiry.

Mirlee glared at her with an expression midway between a pout and a sniff, which made her nose look longer.

"Well, isn't it, *cousin?*" Mirlee demanded.

Teressa smiled and shrugged a little, and sure enough, Mirlee took that as the answer she wanted. She turned to the other girls, saying, "I'm afraid the family looks down on that kind of behavior. She isn't at *all* amusing . . ."

The emphasis on the word *cousin* was to impress the ambassador's daughter, Teressa knew. Mirlee always made certain that girls and boys who had to say "Princess Teressa" would hear her use the family term.

Did it impress anyone? Mirlee was just bending over to pick up another iced cake, and behind her, Baroness Laslan's daughter Kirna was giving Mirlee a venomous look, her round, pleasant face transformed for a moment into something unfamiliar.

Teressa guessed that Mirlee had just aimed at Kirna one of her little remarks about how *fat* the new fashions in lace made some people look.

Kirna hates Mirlee, too, Teressa realized. And unexpectedly, a twinge of pity accompanied a new thought: *I wonder if anyone at all really likes her, or if her followers stay with her just because of her social position and their fear of her tongue.*

Teressa smiled to herself, reflecting again how lucky she was to have a best friend like Wren. *Wren liked me when we were in the orphanage together, and to her the princess business doesn't matter.* Mirlee had sneered at Wren behind her back the one time she'd met her, and said Wren didn't know how lucky she was to have a princess take an interest in a peasant. *But the truth is that I'm the lucky one.*

Rejoicing in her friends, Teressa smiled down at Tyron and patted his head. Casting a quick look at the girls, she saw that they were busy with their talk. "I hope Wren and Connor are all right," she whispered. "Do you think Aunt Leila knows where they are?"

If no one was looking, Tyron usually answered yes-or-no questions with a nod or shake of the head. Teressa waited expectantly, then touched the silky head again. "Tyron?"

The dog looked up at her, his tongue still lolling, then his gaze returned to the insects bumbling lazily among the flowers in the garden.

Someone must have been watching. She straightened up.

Wren and Connor stopped and turned to face one another. "Did you feel that? Somebody tried to scry me."

"Yes." Connor saw Wren clap her hands over her eyes. Two, three long moments passed, then she said, "Whew! I think I closed the inner door, but I'm not sure. I wish I'd had more of that lesson."

Connor felt his scalp prickle. The strange tickle deep inside his head that he knew now for an attempt to scry him had not lasted long. It also hadn't been as strong as the scry attempts he'd felt in the mountains. Still, he found it easy to close it off, now that he knew what it was.

Wren wiped her brow and said, "Shall we get going? The sooner we get to Kiel, the better I'll feel."

Connor voiced agreement, though he felt a tug of regret. Every step he took down the trail diminished his access to magic, and he felt it as a loss. He wanted to go back to the fish-folk, to find out more about his magical side, but they had seemed to think he had things to finish first, and—he reluctantly concluded—they were right. *It is Wren's quest, not mine,* he thought. *But I did promise to return.*

Wren squinted up at the sun, which was now burning brightly on them. Wiping her brow again, she set out at a fast walk. Connor fell into step beside her.

They'd scarcely taken a dozen steps when Wren stopped. This time Connor did not feel anything, but he was not surprised when Wren threw her pack down and went scrambling through it to find her scry-stone.

"Grab me," she said.

Connor touched her arm. At once the "inner door" opened and he saw his half-sister's face.

Leila said, "Someone tried to scry you just now, am I correct?"

"Yes," Wren responded. "But we shut it out."

Leila's mental voice was bright with triumph. "We're closing in, then. Mistress Ferriam has been watching patiently with her stone, and she nearly caught our sorcerous friend."

"Is it the same person who has been causing trouble at court?"

"We believe so. We don't know for certain, but we do have evidence—another magic-made note, this time in a replica of a baron's hand, challenging another baron to a duel. The King has just called a meeting with the barons to explain what is going on. We should be able to end this problem quickly. How about your quest?"

"We'll know something soon," Wren answered.

Listening in, Connor felt Wren's unspoken fears that her journey would produce bad news. He was sure she didn't know that her emotions had leaked out with her mental voice, and so he made sure no answering thoughts of his own gave a clue to his having heard.

"The King will send some of his Scarlet Guard to the border to meet you for your return back. If you need to, hire escort from Allat Los to our border. We may be closing in on the sorcerer here, but we have to be careful."

Connor agreed, and so did Wren. The image faded, and Wren put away her stone. Then she stood up and stretched. "That does tire me," she said.

Connor pointed down the trail. "If we walk quickly, we should get to Kiel well before sunset."

Wren shouldered her pack and they set out once again.

Teressa eased the secret door open just a crack.

She peered through the tiny space, hoping no one in her father's audience chamber below would choose to look up at this particular tapestry. They'd be surprised to see a slit appear in the battle scene, with her eyes staring out.

But she wanted to hear what was going on.

". . . so I'd like you all to pause a moment before you launch into any more feuds, arguments, or challenges. Take the trouble to examine the source of whatever rumor or insult has reached you," her father was saying. His voice had a grim edge as he added, "Cantirmoor is being plagued by this magician, perhaps simply out of malicious enjoyment. Certain of my advisers, however, think there is more serious intent. When we know more, you will be informed."

Teressa could not see her father, but she knew he must have made a gesture of dismissal. She heard the rustle of cloth and the hiss of shoes on marble as the nobles assembled below bowed. The audience was over.

She risked opening the door a little farther and slipped out, wondering if she could catch her father before he went on to his next duty. If she could just get him alone for a moment, she wanted to ask more questions.

Soundlessly she hurried around the narrow balcony. She'd just placed her foot on the winding stairway down when the carved door behind her opened. She whirled around.

"Ah, there you are, Cousin Teressa," said Garian. "I've been looking for you." Behind him was the tall foreigner Hawk. Cousin Nyl lurked by Hawk's broad shoulder.

"What are you doing here?" It was out before she could stop it.

"We were listening from the hallway," Garian said. "We wanted to know what was going on."

Since she'd been doing exactly the same thing, she could hardly fault them for it.

"Where were you?" Garian went on. "I didn't see you on the balcony. Is there another door up here somewhere?"

"I was over there," Teressa said, waving at the other end of the curved balcony.

Garian shrugged and went on, "Well, we agree with the

King." He sent a look to Hawk and Nyl. "There's been too much trouble. It's time for peace."

Teressa would almost have believed them, except for Nyl's smirk. Her years in the orphanage had taught her a lot about the way certain kinds of followers grin when they think their leader is getting away with something.

"That's lovely," she said in her most colorless voice. "Excuse me."

Garian put out his hand to stop her.

"Wait, you haven't heard my idea. We're going to have a picnic. A big one, with lots of great food, and Hawk and I will stand the treats ourselves. We're inviting everyone our age in court, but first we want to know that you'll come. If you come, everyone else will. Come on, say yes," he pleaded. "We'll make it a good one."

Hawk stepped forward and offered her his arm, just like one of the adults would. Teressa did the polite thing and placed her hand on his velvet sleeve, and as he started down the stairs, she kept pace. "We promise to make it something no one will ever forget," he said, smiling down at her.

Teressa studied Hawk for a long moment, trying to gauge that smile. She didn't know him. Though she'd seen him often, he'd never yet paid her the least attention. Now she wondered if that smile was genuine.

For once she dared to drop her bland mask of politeness and gave him one of Wren's favorite sayings. "Is that a promise or a threat?"

It surprised a laugh out of him, an honest one. Behind her, Teressa heard Garian snort in derision, and Nyl snickered.

One of Hawk's dark brows curved upward and he said, "Both. Is that sufficiently intriguing?"

"Yes—" she started.

"Done!" Garian crowed. "Let's go spread the word. We'll have it next week, if the weather looks promising."

"But I didn't—" Teressa began.

135

The boys paid no attention. Garian started talking excitedly to his companions, and they disappeared through one of the archways.

"I didn't say yes," Teressa muttered, then shrugged. She really disliked Garian, but she also remembered what her father had said about getting along with everyone. Besides, maybe a miracle would happen and the party would turn out to be fun.

She remembered her errand then. Dismissing Garian and his party from her mind, she wondered where to search for the King. Then she heard the great gong summoning the household to dinner.

He'll want to change. He hates to sit down in his formal gear and won't do it if he can avoid it. Maybe if I'm fast I can catch him alone. Lifting her skirts, she skimmed quickly over the marble floors toward the other side of the palace.

"Let's run," Wren said as soon as they walked down Kiel's main street. "Did you hear that guard at the city gate say that the Trade Registry closes at sunset?"

"The sun hasn't set," Connor said, squinting upward, "but it's behind the wall, and a lot of these shops are already shutting down."

The same guard that Wren had questioned had provided directions to the Trade Registry. As they dodged among slow carts and laden pedestrians, Wren carefully counted the streets they passed, then sang out, "Tenth!"

"To the left," Connor called back, ducking under someone's arm and skidding out of the way of a prancing horse.

The man riding the horse turned to shout a curse at them, and Connor and Wren exchanged laughs as they ran on.

"Just as well I don't understand Lamreci," Wren called.

"I know a few words, but none of those," Connor said.

This raised another problem, one Wren really hadn't thought about: What if the people at the Trade Registry did not speak any Siradi? She'd had some Allatian language lessons as part of her magician training, but not enough for her to really communicate with anyone.

"How much Lamreci or Allatian do you know?" she asked Connor.

"Little of each," he admitted. "But they supposedly hire folk who are fluent in several tongues. They get caravans from across the Great Desert, after all."

"There it is! And . . . the door is open!" Wren yelled.

They'd emerged from a narrow street into a huge brick-patterned square. Across from them was a vast stone building with heavy doors. As they approached, a man and a woman in black-and-white uniforms came out and began to pull the doors shut.

"Noooo!" Wren yelled, breaking into a run.

Several other people in the square also scurried forward, and Wren and Connor were caught in a crush of people just in front of the doors. Shoved violently from behind by a man bawling something in Allatian, they fell inside the building, and the doors boomed shut behind them.

"We're in!" Connor exclaimed.

"Let's hurry. Records is what we want," Wren muttered. She stopped and gazed with dismay at the confusion of signs and booths spread out in the huge, vault-ceilinged building. "Maybe we should separate, and—"

"This way," Connor motioned.

A sign way off in a corner said in Siradi, *Records,* with words in several different scripts above and beneath it.

Once again they ran, Wren feeling her steps pounding heavily on the hard-packed dirt. They arrived breathless at a counter, just as a thin woman was closing a big book.

She said something unencouraging in Allatian, and Connor stumbled through a reply.

The woman cut in, speaking flawless Siradi: "Why didn't you come in earlier? This will take me time."

"We ran all the way down the mountain," Wren protested.

The woman pursed her lips, giving a faint sniff. "What do you want?"

Wren took out her much-folded, dusty piece of paper. "That baby is me," she said, pointing to the words. "I want to know if any next of kin was listed. If so, where."

"That will cost you twelve silvers, or six Meldrith lil," the woman said uncompromisingly. "First."

Wren winced. Connor counted out the last of the coins in his bag, and Wren added two of hers. The woman accepted them, then said shortly, "Wait here. This'll be a time—the old records are in the lower room." She slammed a book, and disappeared through a curtained-off alcove.

Wren slid to the ground, her back against the wood of the booth.

Connor dropped down beside her.

Wrapping her arms tightly around her knees, Wren wondered where the trail would lead next. If there was any trail. The run down the mountain, the race through the streets, even the woman's discouraging attitude made for a feeling of desperate adventure that could be resolved only in either a total dead end or else a dramatic continuation of the quest. *What happens if the caravan came from across the desert? I can't possibly go there. In fact, I don't know if I can go to the other end of Allat Los . . .*

A step on the other side of the booth made Wren jump to her feet.

The woman showed her a dusty book with worn pages covered in tiny, neat printing.

"Here it is," she said, indicating one of the middle lines. "One baby girl registered."

Wren stared blankly down at the book. "Then there really is someone," Wren whispered.

"Next of kin listed as Nissal Poth, the Two Badgers Inn, Porscan Square," the woman went on.

"Where?" Wren croaked. "What city? What *country*?"

The woman sniffed. "Porscan Square is right by the North Gate."

"It's here? In Kiel?" Wren's head was buzzing strangely, and her feet seemed to be a long way away. "I got my answer." She looked up at Connor. "And it was so easy."

Connor looked back, waiting silently, his eyes questioning.

If it was so easy, why didn't they ever come looking for me?

Chapter Fourteen

*W*ren got out the door somehow. Looking around at the shadowy, unfamiliar buildings, she said, "How do we find Porscan Square?"

"Are you sure about this?" Connor said.

Wren blinked at him. In the fast-fading light he looked worried.

Taking a deep breath, Wren tried to still the seething pit of snakes inside her. "I know what you're thinking," she said, her voice sounding funny to her ears. "So there are relatives. And they didn't come for me. But I'm here, and I have to find out why."

"Then let's go."

Using his stumbling Allatian, Connor asked directions of a girl driving a one-horse cart. Wren waited, fighting against a growing fog of questions.

"This way," Connor said at last.

As soon as they started walking, Wren felt her mind clear a little. She hastily swiped at her hair, hoping she looked tidy enough. Around them, street lighters came out, touching their torches to glass-protected wicks in high lamps.

By the time they reached the square, darkness had fallen and a cold wind was rising. Wren looked over the jumble of peak-roofed shops and houses on the square, then she spotted the inn.

It was a huge, rambling building with ivy-covered walls.

All the windows glowed warm and yellow. Wren and Connor walked under the sign.

At the doorway Connor paused. "Do you want me to wait out here?"

Wren managed to get her voice to work. "It's all right. You'll know soon enough anyway whether or not this is a dead end."

He nodded, opened the door, and they entered a big room filled with tables. It smelled of cinnamon and braised onions and sausage. About half of the tables were filled, mostly with quiet folk wearing the garb of ordinary workers and travelers.

A thickset boy a little older than Wren pushed past, giving them a cursory look. His dark brows contracted when he saw Wren, and he slowed, almost spilling the mugs of ale he was carrying.

"Is Nissal Poth here?" Wren asked in Siradi.

The boy pointed back toward the kitchen. Wren saw a tall man with a bushy gray beard come out carrying a huge pot of steaming soup.

She walked up to him. "Are you Nissal Poth?" she asked.

The man paused in the act of ladling out three bowls of the thick soup, and he frowned down at Wren. "Who wants to know?" he answered back in her own tongue.

"Me," Wren croaked, and handed over her paper.

She wondered if the man could read Siradi. Apparently an innkeeper needed to know a few languages, for he scanned the paper quickly, then looked up at Wren.

In all her imaginings, she'd never expected the reaction she got next. The man's face whitened, and he snapped, "What do you want?"

Wren opened her mouth, but all that came out was a squeak.

Connor stepped to her side, tall and polite. "To meet her relations."

The man's eyes narrowed as he surveyed Connor. "Come with me." He set down his ladle.

Grabbing a lamp off a table, he led the way upstairs, down a hall to the last door, which he opened. Motioning them inside, he set the lamp down on a table, shut the door and stood with his back to it. "What do you want?" he asked again.

Wren felt her eyes blurring. "To find my family—" She stopped and shook her head. She felt behind herself for a stool and sank down onto it.

Beside her Connor spoke again, this time sounding exactly like one of the young aristocrats at court. "My guess is there's a little matter of a disputable inheritance blocking your welcome," he said.

"Huh?" At first Wren was confused. "You mean, I might be a missing heir?"

The man's face changed, this time reddening with anger.

Wren gasped. "I don't—I didn't even know. They just told me the next of kin was one Nissal Poth, who could be found here. So I came."

The man sighed shortly, then pulled a chair to the table. He sat down. Connor continued to stand at Wren's side.

"Who are you?" the man asked. "Both of you. And why are you here?"

"I was raised in Siradayel," Wren said. "And I thought I was an orphan. All I knew was that a boy and I'd been found in the wreckage of a caravan. My search for my family has led me here."

The man's breath hissed in when she mentioned the caravan. "Nissal is my wife," he said finally. "She is—was— sister to Nerin Poth, your mother, who preferred life on the road to tending the inn handed down through her family for nearly three hundred years. Nerin traveled as a caravan guard."

"Nerin was my mother?" Wren said, not bothering any more to wipe the tears from her cheeks.

The man regarded her silently. "Yes," he said at last. "You were born here. You were named for my wife, and until you walked Nissal cared for you. Nerin decided to take you

142

with her that season. The one on which Nerin died was your third trip."

"What about my father?"

The man's face hardened again. "Your father, Arbran, was a worthless fool of a magician who traveled with a motley band of players I always suspected were better thieves than artists. When the Trade Registry sent the message about you, I had it forwarded on to him, but obviously he did not see fit to saddle himself with a child any more than he had when you were a baby."

"Perhaps he never got the message?" Wren gulped.

The man shrugged. "Perhaps. It matters not, as we've never seen him since. He may be dead, for all I know."

"Why didn't my aunt come to get me?"

The man's face tightened.

Connor said, "Because she didn't know, Wren."

The man looked up at him, eyes narrowed. "Who are you?"

"Her friend." Connor gestured to Wren. "And I know a lot about families and inheritances, and people who value the one more than the other."

The man flushed and made a movement toward the door. Wren wiped her eyes hastily, saying, "So my aunt never knew I was alive, is that it?" She sniffed. "Can I meet her? If she doesn't want me, then I'll go away and you'll never see me again."

The man pursed his lips.

"Look," he said finally. "The truth is, the inn is not legally ours, though we've held it together. Nerin promised to sign it over to us, but she always thought it could be done in the future. And then she went and got herself killed. If my wife sees you she'll want to give it to you to bind you here."

"Well, I don't want it," Wren said. "I have a trade of my own. I'm going to be—" She hesitated, remembering what he'd said about her father, then she stated, "a magician. Trained at the Cantirmoor School of Magic," she added with her chin in the air.

143

"I see," he said dryly.

"I just want to meet her. I came because I wanted a family. Not an inn." She sniffed again, even more fiercely.

The man's face reddened again, this time in obvious embarrassment. But he said, "Wait here. I'll have your oath. You might change your mind if you aren't any more successful than—if you aren't successful," he corrected himself hastily. "And we'd lose the only livelihood we have."

He went out, shutting the door firmly behind him.

"Shall we go find the aunt ourselves?" Connor asked.

Wren shook her head, wiping her eyes on her sleeve. "No. I'll do what he wants. I don't care, I just want to meet her."

The man appeared a moment later bearing a pen, a pot of ink, and a roll of blank paper. Everyone was silent as he wrote a line out in two languages, then signed the paper. He handed the pen to Wren.

"Sign as Nissal Poth. Then whatever your new name is."

"Did I get any name from my father?"

The man shook his head. "If he had a family name it's more than we knew. He took the Poth name after the wedding, at least while he was here. I took it, too," he added with self-righteous pride. "There've always been Poths at the Two Badgers."

Wren wrote the name out carefully, thinking: *I came to find out who I am, and I just feel stranger than ever.*

But she had her reward moments after the man took the paper away.

The door banged open, and in sailed a tiny, round lady with bright blue eyes and unruly brown hair escaping from its bun. "Oh, it *is* Neri's baby!" she cried. "Alive. And you look just *like* her!"

Wren gave in at last, her whole body shaking with sobs. But she wept no more loudly than the woman who hugged her so tightly.

———

Teressa looked across the length of the ballroom at the dogs romping in a corner, their claws scrabbling on the smooth marble floor, and laughed. Garian had thrown a ball to keep his new dog from barking, and all of them had gone after it.

"Really," Mirlee exclaimed, her hands on her hips. "Dogs! In a ballroom! Dis-*gusting*."

"Oh, quiet, sourpie," Garian said, striding past her on his way to the dogs. Nyl trotted at his heels, faithful as any of the hounds. "Just because Bouncer doesn't like you."

"Shows good taste," Perd muttered, not quite under his breath, and several boys laughed.

Teressa glanced at Mirlee's scarlet face. "Come, cousin," she said, lifting her voice a little. "Pay no attention to *them*. Let's have a brannel, shall we?"

In the gallery above, the musicians struck up the lively melody of the popular dance. A group of girls formed a big circle, joined by a few of the boys.

To Teressa's surprise, one of the boys who joined the circle was Hawk. He saw her staring, and he smiled at her.

As she whirled around in the first figure of the dance, she glimpsed Garian, Nyl, and Perd still struggling to get the ball away from the tangle of dogs. The boys were laughing almost as loudly as the dogs were yapping. She hoped that they would start a private conversation of the sort she'd over-heard in the rock garden, with Tyron right nearby—but as she turned away she saw Tyron disengage himself from the pile and trot back toward her. During the next figure she saw him sitting obediently at the side, panting gently, his eyes on her.

"That dog of yours is well behaved," said a voice just above her ear. "He seems to like palace life."

Teressa turned to see Hawk next to her, performing his part in the dance with athletic grace. Not wanting any dif-ferences pointed out between Tyron and the real dogs, she said, "He's been here longer—some of them are too new."

"A diverting fashion," he commented. "Dogs at court. They fight less than the humans do in this country."

Stung, Teressa tried to frame a reply that would be polite yet defend Meldrith, but the dance separated them. Hawk moved away, looking back over his shoulder once with a challenging gleam in his dark eyes.

When they met again during the second set, she said, "I notice *you* don't have a dog."

"I do," he replied.

"I haven't met it."

"He hasn't learned obedience yet," Hawk said.

"I wish *some others* would follow your example," Mirlee cut in, throwing a nasty look at Perd, who just then was chasing his dog under the refreshments table.

The dog's plumed tail knocked against a plate of cookies and sent them flying. Garian leaned against the table, his face red with laughter as Perd dived into the mess after his dog, yelling pleas and threats.

The brannel separated all of the dancers again, and Teressa spun away. When she came to that part of the circle once more, Perd had his dog's collar clutched tightly in one hand and with his other he mopped his sweaty face. The table, however, had suffered further attacks, and several people stood nearby looking annoyed.

Teressa was wondering how much longer the dog fashion would last, when several servants came in to clean up the mess. Among them she was surprised to see her mother's maid, dressed just like the others in their gray-and-green livery.

The woman looked up from her task and when her eyes met Teressa's, she brushed the fingers of one hand against her wrist, then returned to her task as if nothing had happened.

The signal for "Come to the study." Alarm burned in Teressa. Just that morning her mother had taught her some of the private signals that she and the King had developed with certain trusted servants. No one ever paid any attention to servants.

Teressa waited until the table was clear, then at a tricky moment during the dance she stepped quite firmly on the hem of her gown.

The ripping sound was loud. "Oh *no!*" Teressa exclaimed, stumbling.

"Princess!" Kirna pointed at Teressa's torn skirt. "How horrid. Would you like me to help you pin it up?"

"Thanks, but I can do it in a trice," Teressa said. "No need for you to miss any fun." She stepped out of the circle. "I'll be right back."

Holding her skirt bunched in one hand, she walked out at a sedate pace. Tyron followed, his toenails clicking on the marble floor. As soon as she'd closed the big doors, though, she ran up the hall. Pressing a latch hidden in a piece of carving, she slipped into a narrow passage and pulled it shut behind her. A tiny glow-globe lit the steep stairs, which she ran up two at a time, the dog right behind her.

She skidded to a halt, breathing fast, when she saw Leila waiting for her. "*There* he is!" Leila exclaimed in relief. "Why didn't he come for his check today? Mistress Ferriam and Halfrid waited for hours!"

"I don't know," Teressa said. "He was gone for a while this afternoon . . ."

They both looked down at the dog, who slowly wagged his tail.

"Well, go in now," Leila exclaimed, sounding exasperated. "Master Falstan is waiting for you in the study. I have to get back to the school. It's been a nightmare."

"My parents?" Teressa gasped.

"They are fine—and surrounded by magicians," Aunt Leila said with a grim smile. "But they are both busy at their peacemaking activities, especially since someone managed to get two of the ambassadors angry this afternoon while we were all waiting—or looking—for Tyron. I have to go," she said, starting for the stairs.

Teressa nodded, continuing on to the study. There she found the tall Master Magician waiting. He greeted her courteously, and without wasting any more time he held a scrystone down near the dog. Tyron gazed up at him, ears flicking back and forth as the magician murmured a spell.

A moment later Master Falstan lowered the stone. "He seems fine," he said, but his forehead was creased with a line of doubt.

"Is something wrong?" Teressa asked, fear making her heart constrict.

"I wish I were better at this than I am," the Master said. "But Ferriam is needed elsewhere, and so is Halfrid. I'll just try it once more." He repeated the spell, and then shrugged. "Tyron seems fine," he said. "The image is quite clear. He just seems . . . distracted."

"He's been a dog for several days," Teressa said. "And I've noticed he doesn't answer me with nods or headshakes anymore. *Tyron.*" She addressed the dog. "Are you all right?"

The dog looked up at her and thumped his tail.

"I think he's probably fine, but the shape-change must be tiring him," the magician said.

"Well, we'd better return to the dance before someone wonders if I'm sewing a new dress," Teressa said, retrieving a tiny packet of pins from an inner pocket. "I'll have to pin this as I walk."

"Goodness, where *does* the time go!" Niss exclaimed, looking out the window at the sun setting over the city wall. "We'll have the dinner crowd here in no time."

"Want me to finish drying these cups, Aunt Nissal?" Wren asked.

"I want you to call me Niss," her aunt exclaimed. "When I hear 'Nissal,' I think I'm in trouble. As for those cups—it would help, but I don't want to leave—oh! I know. I'll bring the apples in here to peel for the pies."

"I can peel as well," Wren said. "And I'll do the cups later. Then we can talk some more."

"There's so much to tell you!" Niss exclaimed. "And so much to show you. How long will you stay?"

Wren sighed. "I'm afraid it can't be as long as I'd like," she admitted. "I've got to get back to my studies, for one thing."

Niss sighed, digging into her sack of apples. "You sound just like your father," she said. "Dear Arbran! He had itch-feet, and no mistake. But we all loved him, for wherever he was, music and laughter weren't far behind. I think it so strange we haven't seen him these ten years! I do hope something terrible hasn't happened."

"Well, if you do hear from him, you'll remember where I am?"

"Magic School, Cantirmoor, in Meldrith," Niss repeated. "As if I could forget! And you, friends with a princess, and all your grand adventures. How proud Neri would be." She took a swipe at her nose with her wrist, then returned to her peeling.

Wren hadn't meant to talk about Teressa, but as she and her aunt had exchanged stories all through the night, one by one her various adventures had come out. They'd both laughed over the funny ones. Niss and she had exactly the same sense of humor, and they'd shared jokes from the very start.

Niss had shown her the little trunk of her mother's things that she had kept. It wasn't much: some clothes, a worn sword that she'd used in her training, a few small pieces of jewelry that Wren's father had brought back from other lands. These, her aunt promised, would be sent to her when Wren had a permanent place to live. But there was also the little sketch that Wren's mother had made of Wren when Wren was a baby. It was crumpled and smudged because, her aunt told her, her mother had taken it along when Wren was left behind during her first year. Niss had insisted that Wren take this drawing, and Wren had accepted it gratefully, folding the yellowed paper carefully into the back of her pack so that it would not get more wrinkled.

There had also been talk about Wren's father. From her uncle's description, Arbran had sounded like a charming but lazy, untrustworthy man. He wasn't even a very good magician—half his illusions failed, leaving his player companions without effects in the middle of their plays. But they'd put up with him anyway.

But according to Aunt Nissal, he was a kindhearted fellow who was so popular it didn't matter that his spells didn't work. When he told stories, nobody needed spells—they saw everything right in their own heads. Wren finally decided to ignore what her uncle said.

Wren hadn't mentioned the paper she'd signed, and she noticed that her uncle hadn't, either. And Cousin Nad stayed out of the way the entire evening, glowering doubtfully at her from time to time. Wren wondered if he was afraid she'd try to take his place.

Connor had remained in his room all night, a light burning under his door. At breakfast he'd looked bleary-eyed but satisfied; he told her he had worked on the play until dawn. "And it's almost finished," he said with pride, fighting yawns.

Her aunt said, "That's enough apples. So come over here and watch me. You ought to learn this recipe. It's been handed down in the family since our sixth greatmother. And it's a *family secret.*"

Wren put down her drying cloth, watching her aunt's small, square hands busy at their task. *I thought this kind of work would be boring,* Wren thought, breathing in the scents of fresh apple and cinnamon. *But it's not. It's so peaceful here, despite Cousin Nad and his sourpickle face lurking around corners. It must be nice to have home and work all in one place.* For a moment she felt a twinge at having signed it all away so readily, but when she looked up at her aunt, she knew it was worth it. *I'll visit when I can,* she promised herself. *And help out, and enjoy having a family. Maybe I can even get Nad used to me enough to quit scowling. But the truth is, I do have itchfeet, and I want adventure more than I want to inherit an inn.*

The door opened behind them, and both looked up, startled. Connor stood there, his face pale and his gray-blue eyes dark. "Wren," he said, "I think we have to leave."

"Oh, not yet," Wren protested. "We promised to hire an escort first—"

Then she became aware of the clatter of riding boots on the wooden floor out front. Few of the regular customers at the Two Badgers wore them.

Connor turned away without a word. Wren and her aunt followed.

Her uncle and cousin stood by the counter, staring at the new arrivals, whose blue uniforms Wren recognized with a pang.

The leader, the man with reddish hair, said formally, "We're here to escort Prince Connor Shaltar and Magician Prentice Wren back to Cantirmoor, on orders of Duke Fortian Rhismordith."

"Oh!" Niss said, plumping down onto a chair.

Cousin Nad stared from Wren to Connor, his mouth open, and the fireplace iron he'd been carrying dropped from his fingers straight onto his foot.

Chapter Fifteen

*T*yron tried to stretch, but the bars of his cage pressed against his bones. His tongue moved thickly in his mouth. His body ached, and hunger gnawed at his insides.

I am not a dog, he thought. I am Tyron ner-Halfrid and I WILL escape from this.

He'd been crammed into some kind of wire container that was too small for his body, and around him was continual darkness. He had to rely on his sense of smell for information. So far he'd found out little.

Once a day he was given a little food and water, just enough to keep him alive but not to relieve the terrible thirst or hunger for long. *I know why: It's to make my dog body so miserable my human mind won't be able to think. But I won't give in.*

As near as he could figure, the food was brought in very late at night. The air that came in with whoever brought the food smelled damp and cold, not like the air of daytime.

Whoever it was sometimes spoke, but always in a soft whisper that made it nearly impossible to recognize the voice. And some kind of magic masked the magician's personal scent.

And if I'm right, the next visit should be soon, Tyron thought. At least, I hope so. I don't know how much longer I can go without water.

He shut his eyes, but he warded off sleep, for that was

dangerous. In his dreams he was a dog, and he always awoke disoriented. Time was his enemy now. If this went on for many more days, the chances were ever greater that he would wake up as a dog and never remember anything else.

How did Wren do it last year? She too went long in the dog shape, and Halfrid said she resisted the changeover better than anyone he knew of. How I wish we'd talked about it more.

Still, any kind of thinking was good. Especially thinking about his friends. He sent his mind back, reliving the adventures that they had all shared.

Then a door opened, and the Voice interrupted him.

"How's the mighty journeymage?"

Soft, acid laughter accompanied it. A swirl of air drifted into Tyron's cage, and he sniffed it surreptitiously. *Still the masking spell. But you'll forget one day, and I will know who you are.*

"Nothing to say?"

Now Tyron smelled water, and he licked his chops, his nose running.

The Voice laughed again as Tyron fell on the saucer of water, slurping every drop. Then he licked his paws in case any had fallen onto them.

"Only a few days more, then you'll meet your new master."

Tyron whiffled. *More water. I need more—no. Listen.*

"What? You're not happy? You'll soon have company. Not that any of *you* will be pleased with your new home. But my esteemed ally Andreus will be pleased. He remembers his friends, journeymage, and he also remembers those who dare to strike against him."

The Voice laughed again, and Tyron heard a shifting of cloth.

Come closer. Let me smell what else you've brought in here, find out where you've been, he thought. He let out a soft whine: *Come closer.*

"What's the matter, afraid? Ah, but this is gentle compared to the life you will soon have. And it *will* be soon. In a way it's a shame, for we'll miss the fun here. But your fool of a king has obligingly cleared his Scarlet Guard away from my home at last, and there's work to be done."

Tyron sniffed, long and delicately. Herb scent, from the palace garden. And the sharp smell of the stable. And—

"Nothing to say? You are not very exciting company." The mocking voice paused, then something dropped into the cage. "Here's your feast. Enjoy." Then came the sound of a door closing.

Tyron fell on the dried meat, finished it quickly, then he licked his paws. *I have to get free!* He turned his attention once more to exploring every fraction of his cage.

Wren stared out of the tent flap and sighed.

Everything was a mess.

Between the drifting fingers of fog, she could just make out Connor's tent. The Blues had given him one alone, and he sat there, still and quiet. He hadn't spoken a word to anyone since they'd left Kiel. Each time they stopped to eat he buried himself in working on his play, or else he just sat and stared, like now. Because he was a prince, the Blues respectfully left him alone, and Wren was tired of trying to get him to talk, for even when she addressed him, he answered in polite monosyllables.

Wren shared a tent with a Blue named Kari. The older girl had been hesitant to talk to her at first, particularly when Connor had frozen them all out with his dignified silence. But Wren had tried hard to overcome Kari's shyness. At night Kari studied languages by candlelight, and Wren had offered to help her study verb forms. Kari finally told Wren that she planned to be a courier. To get into their guild she had to know six tongues.

Right now Kari had sentry duty. Dawn was just breaking over the quiet camp. Usually everyone was awake, or waking, by now, but today they seemed to want to sleep in. And no wonder: the fog was thickening steadily in the chilly air, blocking the weak sunlight coming over the towering peaks.

Wren wrapped herself more securely in her cloak, thinking hard.

She'd wakened suddenly, alarmed in her dream by the feeling that a magic attack of some kind was about to happen, but the camp was quiet. Nothing had changed.

She certainly had enough to think about. First, trying to figure out whether or not they were prisoners. Nobody had said anything, but they were never out of the Blues' sight. She also needed to ponder her visit in Kiel. *I can't think of myself as Nissal Poth or as a born citizen of Allat Los. I don't even speak the language,* Wren thought. Still, she did like the idea of being a citizen of three lands. That had the right ring to it for a future adventurer . . .

Aunt Nissal had said, "I guess it was fated you'd get Neri's wanderlust, and that you'd turn to magic studies, like your father."

Wren wasn't sure how she felt about this assumption. *As if I've not made any choices at all in what I've done.* Wren knew she could just as easily have picked half a dozen other jobs and been happy. Also, she knew she had a talent for scrying, but no one had mentioned either of her parents having such a talent. *I'm me, not them.*

She looked out, her vision blurry. She could barely see Connor's tent now, an indistinct shape in the white fog. Sleepiness stung her eyelids, but she fought against it. Soon everyone would arouse and they'd be riding again, and she'd lose her chance to think.

At least now I know where I come from. Wren laughed at her old dreams: the long-lost child of some queen or emperor. She knew now she had parents and family, even a real birthday. And it was worth the frowns of ten Cousin Nads, just to have met Aunt Niss!

Her eyes drooped, but she forced them open. She knew she shouldn't be sleepy; she'd had a good night's rest. Yet her eyelids burned, tempting her to close them.

I know. I'll visit Kari.

Wren forced herself to her feet, and as she walked the drowsiness slipped away.

To her surprise, Kari was not walking briskly back and forth on guard duty. She sat on a boulder, chin in hands, eyes closed. Not far distant, Wren saw a slumped silhouette that she took to be the other sentry. He appeared to be sound asleep.

"Kari?" Wren said.

Kari started and sat up. "Wren! Where'd you come from?"

"Our tent. This fog is something, isn't it?"

"I guess so." Kari yawned. "Funny. Usually I don't get so tired on early-morning watch," she said dreamily.

Wren hesitated, her thoughts distracted by two separate subjects. Her first thought was, *Why is she so tired?* Wren fought a yawn, forcing her mind to the most immediate problem. So far, no one had mentioned the circumstances under which the Blues had chased through two countries to find them. *Maybe this sort of thing isn't done, but I've got to know.*

"Kari, what does the Duke want with us?"

Kari yawned again. "Doesn't," she said. "His heir sent us." She looked up at Wren with heavy eyes. "You know, we were all wondering. Why did Prince Connor run off in the first place?"

"Huh?"

"He knocked the Duke's heir down," Kari said patiently. "That's what we were told. Prince Connor was supposed to appear before the King to explain, but he ran off. So we were sent to bring him back."

Wren sucked in a deep breath, forgetting all her tiredness. The fog swirled closer, making the world seem unreal.

"Is that what you were told?"

"It's the truth," Kari said. "At first we were told he'd been sent to the lake, but someone found out he never got there. So he must have run away! Maybe he had his

156

reasons—I know what Lord Garian's temper is like—but it's only right to have a hearing when those things happen. Then both sides get to speak. But Prince Connor shouldn't have run off." Her voice took on color for a moment, and the drowsiness faded from her eyes.

Wren thought rapidly, then said: "Kari, can you tell me how many times you got close to us?"

"We never did. What a run! First back and forth along the Northwood road, then we finally got word that you'd left the country. So we went to Pelsir, to see if they knew of you there. Sure enough, you'd been there and had just left two days before. Since we had the proper papers, the Siradi Browns gave us the word we'd find you somewhere in Kiel, or if not there, we were to check with the Trade Registry." She shrugged. "It wasn't very exciting, really. Still, after such a long trip, it was a relief when we finally reached the city and there you were." She yawned a third time. "You know . . . I feel a little dizzy . . . Would you mind if I just put my head down?"

She cradled her head on her arms, and then Wren heard a gentle snore. Kari was asleep. And something was wrong with that sleep.

Wren drew in a deep breath, fighting the descending drowsiness again—and a familiar feeling buzzed in her mind. It was subtle, no more than the hum of a tiny insect heard on a breeze, but inside her head: *Magic.*

Alarm burned through her, leaving her thoroughly awake.

She turned and stumbled back toward the camp. Even though it was only a few steps away, the thick fog confused her, and she bumped against several tents before she found hers. No one protested—no one was awake.

She faced the direction she knew Connor's tent lay in. "Connor?" she whispered. "Something's wrong."

She crossed the space between their tents. The fog was thickest here, and she almost tripped over Connor before she saw him. The inner tingle of magic was stronger than ever.

157

Connor was sitting very straight in the middle of his tent, his eyes closed. He was not asleep; he was sitting too rigidly for that.

"Connor?"

He jumped. "Wren!"

"What's—" Wren gasped. "That magic—it's *you* doing it."

"I wish you'd fallen asleep with the rest of them." His voice was hoarse with strain. "Don't try to stop me."

"From what?"

"From leaving."

Connor got up, reached for his pack, then staggered. He sat down again abruptly. "*Hoo,*" he breathed. "I'd forgotten how that magic does take one's stuffing out."

"Why are you leaving? I don't understand."

"I won't go back to Cantirmoor as a criminal," Connor said. "I've had enough of them all. I've done nothing wrong, and—"

Wren was ordinarily a peacemaker, but when she realized what a close call they'd just had, she exclaimed with heartfelt exasperation: "I know that, you *weedwit.*"

Connor gave her a startled look. "Pardon?"

"Oh! And to think you almost—argh! You *could* have asked them, instead of ignoring everyone and working on that dratted play, looking at them like they were bugs whenever they came near, *just* like some fool of a hero in a very stupid song. They came after us because they think we ran away!"

"I don't understand," Connor said, shaking his head hard.

"Remember that business in the garrison courtyard, when everyone thought you hit old cheesenose Garian? Well, Garian seems to have sent them because he thought we escaped from the King's justice and ran off. So he's bringing you back for that."

Connor thumbed his eyelids.

"I guess it didn't work, our trying to keep our departure

secret," Wren went on, "but since the *King* knows what really happened, don't you think it will take the space of *ten words* to straighten it all out?"

"But the fire, those people after—"

"Wasn't these Blues," Wren said. "Which you could have found out if you'd *talked* to them. I don't think they're lying. In fact, I have proof: the fellows the Commander captured didn't have some kind of official search papers. But these Blues, who showed up after we left, brought papers along with them. That's why the Pelsir people sent them after us."

"So . . . we're being chased by two sets, is that it?" Connor asked.

Wren nodded. "And you know who sent the second group."

"The magician who scryed us. But Garian is allied with him, we already figured that."

"Maybe," Wren said doubtfully. "Whew, your fog magic makes it hard to think! But I'm sure of this: The King and the magicians aren't against us. Nor are these people our enemies. I think we'd better explain just what's going on. They may be able to help us."

Connor dropped his pack and sighed. "I was going to put everyone to sleep and go back to the fish-folk. No one would get hurt trying to stop me, but I'd be where I seem to belong."

"Except you *don't* belong with them. Not yet, anyway. Didn't they say you had something to finish first? Besides, if you went back now, you'd just be out there alone for that nasty magician to find."

Connor studied his hands in silence, then he looked up. "I've been trying to convince myself that the fish-folk just meant *your* quest has to be finished. It doesn't matter whether I'm there or not."

Wren said, "I think they meant that *both* of us will be needed in Cantirmoor."

Connor thought about that a moment, then nodded solemnly. "You're right."

"Then get rid of your fog," she said. "Before I curl up and snore for a week."

Connor laughed. "Gladly. Besides, I can't hold it any longer."

And I couldn't do something like this even for a moment, Wren thought. *One mystery is cleared up, but Connor's magic is always going to remain a mystery.*

"Wren?"

"Huh?" She gave a huge yawn.

"Thanks."

I know who you are, Tyron thought. *I've got to tell someone.*

Tyron collapsed against the unforgiving wire, exhausted. The gloating Voice had forgotten the masking magic. Or had deliberately left it off.

"In two days I win," the Voice had whispered, coming no closer than the doorway—checking that Tyron was still there, still alive. "And in two days you go to Senna Lirwan." Then the door closed.

And Tyron, sniffing, recognized the foreigner Hawk.

Tyron lunged desperately, trying to tip his cage over. *No way out,* he thought in despair. *Not even if I chew my teeth down to nothing—I can't break through this wire. There must be another way.*

He thought longingly of his scry-stone. Not that he was that good with it, but he knew that people in trouble sometimes focused better than they did when scrying for a school exercise.

Though he didn't have a stone, the darkness had helped to shut everything else out—and still neither Leila nor Mistress Ferriam, who taught scrying at the school, had heard him.

If only one of them were not so good at closing off her mind to scry access. If only he knew someone who couldn't close off but who knew scrying—

Wren!

He let out a sharp yip.

She was a long distance away, he had no idea where. And he had no stone. Could he do it?

Well, he was about to find out.

Chapter Sixteen

"Come join the dance, Princess," Hawk said to Teressa, sweeping a practiced bow.

Teressa surveyed Garian's friend, smiling politely. "I was just about to take a breather," she said. "I've just danced six in a row."

"Good." He smiled and sat down beside her. "I'll join you."

She studied his strong-boned face. The smile seemed genuine, his dark eyes gleaming in the light of the hundred candles that brightened the ballroom. He was tall and broad-shouldered and seemed a lot older than Garian or Nyl or the others. Maybe he wasn't a grown-up yet, but he looked like one. Something nagged at Teressa: Why did Hawk spend his time with Garian if he was in Meldrith to learn diplomacy?

"What's Fil Gaen like?" she asked.

"Fil Gaen?" he asked.

"Isn't that where your home is?"

"Near enough," he said. "What is it you want to know?"

She gave her head a little shake, feeling slightly disconcerted. Unlike the other boys, who expressed boredom, or anger, or laughter, or scorn so readily, his expression was impossible to read.

"Hawk doesn't talk about his place," a familiar voice cut in. "If that's what you're asking."

Garian dropped down by Teressa's other side. Unlike

Hawk, who wore plain dark blue velvet, Garian was brilliantly dressed, his scarlet tunic gleaming with jewels. A long knife in a gold-covered sheath poked Teressa's leg when he sat down. Garian didn't notice, not even when Teressa put out a hand and gave the weapon a push.

"His holding is bigger than any of ours," Marit put in, joining them.

Hawk gave a shrug. "Would you want to talk about a place someone else is sitting on and won't hand over to you, even though it's yours?"

"A regent is holding onto your property?" Teressa asked.

Hawk gave a nod. "And I'm not strong enough—yet—to throw him out."

"Perhaps you could speak to my father about it?" she suggested hesitantly.

"Well, that's why I'm here," he said. "But these things take time. And as long as the time has some fun in it, I don't mind much." He grinned.

Garian prodded her arm to get her attention. "What games d'you like best, cousin?" he asked. "For the picnic."

Teressa hesitated, thinking: *None of the ones you play.* But she wasn't going to say that out loud.

"Stickle-ball?" Nyl suggested, hovering behind the others.

"Not at a party, dolt," Garian said scornfully.

"Treasure hunt?" Perd put in, behind Marit's shoulder.

"That's so-oo much work," Marit groaned.

"When I was your age I liked hide-and-find best," Hawk said to Teressa.

She smiled. "That's fun."

"Aw, that's for babies," Garian snarled.

"Not if you play in teams," Hawk said. "And take hostages—"

"Hostages!" Garian exclaimed. "That's fun."

"You have to write ransom notes, and the others either have to pay ransom or else track their missing teammates," Hawk continued.

Garian chortled. "Now that sounds more like it."

"And it has to be proper language," Hawk said. "You know, not, 'Hand over three bags of gold or we croak your pal.' More like, 'We hand you our challenge, an ye dare to meet it. We hold your fair princess—' "

Garian cut in, "I know! 'We do promise to do grievous harm to our hostage lest ye surrender unto us the demands herewith listed.' Oh, like those old-fashioned plays. I know—as if all my grandfather's old letters weren't just like that. The times my tutor made me copy them out, to make my handwriting better! Never thought that I'd be able to use them."

"We'll plan it, then," Hawk said. "If it suits you?" he asked Teressa.

The boys chimed in eagerly, and she laughed. "If everyone else wants to," she said.

Garian jumped up. "Great! Let's go lay some plans. This dancing stuff is dull as ditch water."

He jabbed Perd, and they hurried off. Hawk stood up, placed his hand over his heart in an elegant bow, and moved after them more slowly.

While a relieved Teressa watched the boys go off seeking fun, Wren was sound asleep high in the mountains overlooking Meldrith. She and Connor had spent the long day talking things over with Kari and the Blues, first explaining what had happened to them, then listening to the Blues' story.

Around the campfire at dinner, Wren, Connor, and the Blues agreed that they should hurry back to Cantirmoor as quickly as possible and try to get to the King before anyone else saw them.

Wren had gone to sleep in a good mood, satisfied that things would work out after all. But she fell straight into a nightmare.

In the dream Tyron was trying to find her, but he couldn't

see anything. He kept calling to her, his voice dry and desperate-sounding.

She groaned, turning in her sleep to escape.

"Wren!"

Wren's eyes opened. She saw Kari looming over her, dark hair tousled. Pale light from both moons lit the side of Kari's worried face.

"Are you all right?"

Wren shook her head, half caught in the dream still. "Tyron," she muttered. The dream shards drifted away, but real worry took its place. "Something's wrong with him."

"What?" Kari said.

"It's all right," Wren said, waking up completely. "Thanks."

Kari lay back down, and Wren waited until her breathing was deep and even, then she quietly reached into her pack and took out her scry-stone. She knew she was not supposed to be scrying, but she had to check.

I'll just hope it's one of our people I catch, and not that sorcerer. She closed everything else out of her mind and tried to raise an image of Mistress Leila in her glass.

Almost immediately she saw color glow deep in the stone, and then Mistress Leila frowned at Wren, her displeasure clear. "Emergency?"

"No. At least, not for us. I had a bad dream—about Tyron, and I wondered—"

Mistress Leila's face cleared. "I saw him just before sunset. He was running around the park with the rest of the pack."

"What?"

Mistress Leila laughed. "It was your idea, Wren. He's a dog, spying out the spider in the palace walls."

Wren choked on a laugh, sending a hasty glance at Kari.

"If he's all right, then I won't worry."

"He is. And Wren—"

"I know. Don't scry. I won't again. We should be back in a day or so anyway."

Mistress Leila's image winked out; she'd closed off.

Wren slid the stone back into her bag and lay down in relief.

Everything was fine . . .

But she had the dream again.

Just before dawn the next day, Connor yanked his soggy cloak more closely about him, trying not to shiver. Mud splashed up from his horse's hooves, splattering the sides of his legs. The steady rain drummed on his head and shoulders and back.

He looked once to see how Wren was faring. Her face was grim in the gloomy predawn light—just like Connor felt.

Their group had traveled hard and fast through a long day and a night, and everyone was tired. Connor in particular, but he could not complain. The fish-folk had warned him against using his weather magic, but he'd been too angry to heed them. As a result of his sleep-fog he'd been terribly drained, but there had been no chance to rest long enough to recover. The fast pace the Blues set took all the rest of his strength.

Now, scarcely an hour's ride from Cantirmoor, he had to pinch himself hard, fighting against a lassitude heavier than the magical sleep he'd tried to put on the others. He knew that if he relaxed for a moment, he'd fall off his horse and never wake up.

"This way," Master Hallig called out, waving to the south.

After another long space, during which the weak sun grayed the eastern clouds, the Blues pulled up in neat rows on top of a gentle hill. Tiredly, Connor lifted his head, to see not far away the familiar arched windows and tall pillars of the royal palace at Cantirmoor, golden-lit from within.

"We will enter through the park," Hallig said. "In this weather and this early, the only people we're likely to en-counter will be the King's Guard, and we can trust them to keep mum." He paused and looked over at Connor with the air of someone waiting.

Connor knew he needed to express appreciation. He forced his mouth open, trying to gather the energy to speak.

Wren beat him to it. "We are truly grateful, Master Hallig. And you'll soon see that we told you the truth."

Connor cast Wren a thankful look as Hallig smiled.

"Come, then," he said. "Let's make an end to this journey, and get to some hot food and a dry place by the fire."

They began riding again, and Connor straightened up in his saddle, thinking, *Just a little longer. Just a little farther.*

Wren rode beside him still. He saw her head swinging this way and that, her heavy, wet braid thumping her cloak. *Watching for evil magicians?* Connor was too tired to care.

They rode straight to the palace in the hard rain, stopping directly behind the royal wing.

There Master Hallig, Wren, and Connor dismounted. The other Blues took the horses away and disappeared in the gloom.

A tall, gaunt figure appeared with a lamp, and Connor recognized with relief the familiar features of Helmburi, the King's steward. If Helmburi were here, then everything must be all right.

Greeting Master Hallig with a word, Helmburi bowed to Connor. "You'll find the King and Queen at breakfast. Come along with me."

Connor felt the world tilt slightly as he walked after Helmburi. Wren shot him a glance of concern and moved close by. "Are you all right?"

"Tired."

Wren pursed her lips. Before she could answer, a light voice greeted them: "Wren!"

Connor looked up wearily, to see Teressa fly down the marble steps and grab Wren in a big hug. Graceful in her embroidered gown, she didn't seem to notice Wren's dripping clothing.

167

Wren laughed and backed away. "Now look, you're all wet."

"I don't care, it's just so *good* to see you home," Teressa said. Then she turned to Connor, and he could almost feel her effort. "Welcome home, cousin."

She'd remembered not to call him *uncle*, at least. Too tired to think of something polite to say, he just returned her nod, and her brow contracted slightly. Then she turned away. "Let's go to my room and talk."

Connor watched them disappear down a hall, Wren's voice drifting back, ". . . and I *found* them! Oh, and you will love my Aunt Niss . . ."

Connor felt a touch on his arm. "Connor?"

It was Astren, looking at him with a searching concern.

"What's wrong, my boy?" That was King Verne.

Master Hallig was nowhere in sight. How much time had passed? Connor rubbed aching eyes and shook his head.

It's the magic, it must be the magic, he thought. But his mind did not produce a memory of his magical experiences. Instead he saw the look in Teressa's eyes when she saw Wren, and how that glow had dwindled to wary politeness when she turned to face him.

Verne clapped him on the shoulder. "You're tired. Well, I'll have something hot brought in. Then we will talk. And after that you'll sleep, right here in our apartments. By tomorrow we should be able to solve most of our mysteries, and until that time no one is going to see you."

"Here," Astren said, pressing a warm cup of fresh cocoa into his hands. "First, drink." She turned to the King. "I will go warn the girls that Wren is to remain up here today."

"Will you talk to Hallig?" the King asked. After the Queen nodded and moved away, Verne turned back to Connor. "Now. Let's hear it. Everything that happened."

Everything that happened—except the magic. Not yet.

Connor took a deep breath.

168

As soon as the two girls got to Teressa's room, the Princess slammed the door shut and whirled around to face Wren. "Tyron's missing."

Wren stared, trying to comprehend the words. She knuckled her tired eyes. "Missing?"

Teressa bit her lip. "The sorcerer substituted another dog—we don't know when. Our magicians were fooled until yesterday."

"Yesterday . . . " Wren repeated. "Was that when I scryed Mistress Leila? No, that was the night before. But she said he was well—"

Teressa gave her head a shake. "That's what the magicians thought. There is an illusion on the real dog, a very clever one, they said. But after she got your message, they went to check him again. They were worried anyway, for he had been in that shape so long, and I guess there was something odd about his image in their scry-stone—always exactly the same. This time they used some special kind of magic to check, and that dog wasn't Tyron."

"So where is he?"

"No one knows," Teressa said. She looked tense and tired, as if she had not slept, either. "And now I have to go to this picnic and pretend that nothing is wrong."

"Picnic?" Wren said, and she forced a grin. "I'm sorry to sound like an echo, but I'm confused. How can you go to a picnic with Tyron missing?"

Teressa explained quickly about Garian's picnic, adding, "The grown-ups are having a party of their own, at the Eth-Lamrec ambassador's place. Everyone is going to go, including some suspicious foreigners that the magicians have been watching."

"Do the magicians think some kind of magic is going to be done at the ambassador's?"

"They didn't talk much about the details, but they said they traced some kind of magical preparations—this is one of the reasons why they couldn't find Tyron. There are too few of them, too many nasty traps they've had to find and

169

spring, and of course they have to protect Mother and Father. They have been *desperate*. Anyway, they figure something will happen at that party today. So all of them but Aunt Leila will be there to help. She's going to watch over the park, just in case anyone would try to get around all the magic protections over it and try some trick with *us*."

"*Hoo*," Wren said. "Wish there was a way to sneak along to the ambassador's and watch what happens. Once we catch that sorcerer, we should find Tyron easily."

"I know," Teressa said, looking grim. "I'd like to help catch this villain, too. Instead I have to go to Garian's party. Well, they promised to tell me about it if their plan works—and then we can join the search for Tyron." She glanced at her colored candle, then said, "I guess I had better get ready."

The two girls walked into Teressa's dressing room. As Teressa started rummaging through her trunks, Wren said, "So they are sure that the rumors and the problems were all caused by one sorcerer?"

"They are not sure of anything," Teressa said. "Except that they have laid enough magical traps at the ambassador's place to catch the Emperor of Sveran Djur himself. No one will get by them there."

"But what about Tyron?" Wren said, feeling sick inside. "If they *don't* catch the sorcerer, all this villain has to do is keep Tyron somewhere until the dog instinct takes over the human completely."

"Halfrid blames himself for permitting Tyron to try the shape-change. He's worked harder than anyone—I don't think any of the magicians have slept in three days," Teressa said from the depths of a ribbon-trimmed velvet gown. Her head emerged, and she smiled sympathetically. "I'm sorry, Wren. I've scarcely let you talk—you found your family?"

"Yes," Wren said. "I'm a Poth," she said, trying for lightness. "Innkeepers for centuries. My aunt—" She sagged in her chair, shaking her head. "Oh, I'll tell you later. I'm sorry, I can't get Tyron out of my head. I had nightmares about him every night, and now I know why."

Silence fell between them for a moment, Teressa looking grim as she fixed pearls in her long auburn hair.

Now she has to go out and socialize, pretending nothing's wrong. "Your hair looks pretty like that, with pearls braided in it," Wren said.

Teressa surveyed herself critically in the mirror, then gave Wren a wry smile. "I feel just like one of the stage players, preparing for the part of the carefree princess. But look!" She pulled up her skirts and, in the calmest way possible, slid a slim-bladed little knife into the top of her velvet-covered walking boots.

"What's that for?"

"Nothing, I hope. But I made myself a promise last year that I'd never be taken defenseless again. It makes me feel better to go out with that little knife, even in our own park." She turned a lopsided little smile on Wren. "Mama gave it to me."

Wren grimaced. "Well, I hope all you use it for is to stab your peas—"

A knock sounded at the door, and Queen Astren came in.

"Is it already time to go?" Teressa asked.

"It is, daughter," the Queen said, then turned to Wren. "We think it would be best if you remain here in the palace until this day is ended. Everyone thinks you and Connor are still on your journey."

Wren nodded. "Yes, ma'am," she said.

Teressa hugged her again. "I'll be back as soon as it's polite to leave," she said. "And we'll talk more then."

Chapter Seventeen

*I*n the guest room near the King's suite, Connor's fingers played with his pen as he stared down at his papers.

Done.

His play was finished and revised to his satisfaction, but he felt no joy in it. Ordinarily his escape when things around him made him unhappy, it wasn't enough now.

His eyes went to the window as he thought about what the King had told him. Tyron—missing, imprisoned in the form of a hound.

Just then he heard a slight tapping sound—footsteps. Dropping his pen onto the papers, he went to the door and looked out in time to see a shadow flicker down one wall and round a corner.

Moving to that corner, he peered around. A girl in an ill-fitting servant's gown looked to both sides, then slipped inside the King's study. Connor waited, not sure what to do. The girl reappeared almost immediately and ran full speed in the other direction.

Connor moved up the hall to the King's study. As he passed the Queen's sitting room, he peered inside and saw his half-sister Leila seated at the table with her head cradled in her arms. Next to her was a golden cup. He was going to ask if she'd seen anything, when he realized she was deeply asleep.

He knew what it felt like to be that tired. Backing up,

he went on down toward the King's study. He opened the door and cast a quick look around, not sure what to expect. His eyes lit on a paper lying on the clean, smooth desk. Connor picked it up and ran his eyes down it in growing surprise.

I have the Honor of Informing You that the Princess Teressa lies in Durance Vile at a Location Unknown to You. If you Wish to See her Again, you Shall comply with the following Demands . . .

And a list of enormous sums, plus land, was named.

And at the bottom, signed with a flourish, was the name *Garian Rhismordith.*

Connor crammed the note into his pocket and ran down the stairs as fast as he could. His first thought was to get to the ambassador's house as soon as he could. The idea of retribution lent him speed. "Oh, you idiot, Garian," he muttered as he raced down the marble stairs, skidded around a corner, and started down the hall toward the stable. "*Now* they'll see—"

See what?

Connor slowed, stopped. Running his eyes down the paper again, he shook his head. Something was wrong.

Magic? He remembered the paper in his own handwriting that the Master Magician had found. *But Garian doesn't know magic. So his friend the sorcerer does . . . His friend?* Garian remembered Master Hallig and the Blues. They hadn't known anything about the other group searching for Connor and Wren. Was it possible Garian had not known, either?

Connor shook his head again. Something was definitely wrong. Garian was a pain, and obnoxious, but Connor was fairly sure he was no traitor. A game, maybe? But that didn't make sense either; no one who knew about Teressa's disappearance last year would take this as a joke. Especially a joke played on the King.

Connor looked out the door, unsure what to do, then

he thought of Wren. Turning around, he raced back upstairs and burst into Teressa's room.

Wren was seated near a window, her scry-stone in her hand. She looked up, her eyes confused for a moment.

"Wren?"

"Look at this," Wren said, pointing to the stone. "It really is an evil spell."

Connor came forward, still holding the paper, and looked into her stone. He saw a brown dog with a green ribbon tied round its neck. It lay in the sunny stableyard with several other dogs, gently panting.

"That's what comes when you do the magical summons spell. But when I try to call him *here*"—she smacked her forehead—"I get this dark, horrible feeling. I can't figure it out."

Connor sighed. "First, look at this. You can tell me: Is this paper magicked? You know, a fake?"

"You can't tell?" Wren asked as she thrust her scry-stone into the pouch at her side.

Connor shrugged. "It feels like nothing but paper to me."

Wren took it, and shut her eyes, rubbing her fingers along the edge. "It's real," she said, then scanned it. Her eyes widened suddenly, and she gaped at Connor. "Is this *true?*"

"That's what I'm trying to figure out. It just doesn't seem right somehow." He told her about the servant dropping it in the King's study.

"Did you show it to Mistress Leila?"

"She's asleep," Connor said. "But this is important. We'll have to wake her up."

They rushed out together, crossing the hall to the Queen's room.

"Leila," Connor said.

She didn't move.

"Mistress Leila, we need . . . " Wren began.

The magician did not even stir.

Wren grabbed her shoulder and shook her, and Leila's head rolled loosely, her deep breathing undisturbed.

"This is bad," Wren said, straightening up. "Either she's enchanted or else someone put something nasty into that cup. What now?"

"We have to find help," Connor said. "But without being seen. In case that servant is spying around."

"But what about Tyron?" Wren said. "That darkness scares me—"

Connor's eyes went to the big scry-stone resting near Leila's fingers. As Wren said Tyron's name, Connor had seen a flicker deep in the stone, and he'd felt a sharp jab right behind his eyes. Fear, pain, urgency flooded his mind, and with them a whispering of thought, just out of reach.

Shoving the paper into his pocket, he sat down. "How do you work this thing?" He grabbed Leila's scry-stone.

Wren muttered a spell, touching the stone. At once the flicker resolved into the illusion showing the dog in the stable-yard. Connor blinked, putting his hands over the stone.

"Not that way," he said. "It doesn't work for me." He shut his eyes, reaching with his mind, calling to his friend: *Tyron.*

Again he felt that jab and the swift rush of emotions and whispered thoughts. Opening his eyes, he said to Wren, "I'm not strong enough. Maybe if I were in the mountains . . . but I'm not. You try with me. Do your spell, but don't look at that stone. Look *here.*" He tapped his forehead.

Wren whispered the words of her scry-spell, and for a moment there was silence. Then Connor felt the jab once again, and Wren exclaimed, "He heard me—"

"That way," Connor said, feeling an inner tug pulling him northward. He pointed at the north wall.

Wren pressed her lips together into a line, her light blue eyes intent. "Let's go. We'll find Tyron first, and then take care of that paper."

Moving silently, they checked around the corners before they entered the hallway. Pausing only for occasional servants to pass, they ran down through the palace until they came out onto a terrace. Once more they both worked together to call Tyron, and the inner tug pulled Connor again.

He started walking slowly, stopped, then started in another direction, this time at a faster pace. Wren stayed beside him, silent and watchful.

No one disturbed them as they moved toward the older buildings behind the stable, then past them to the edge of the park and beyond. Connor led them around the edge of an old quarry, then stopped to stare at a broad, empty field.

"It's here," he said at last.

"Can't be," Wren exclaimed, waving her hand. "There's nothing here but grass."

"He's got to be here—somewhere," Connor said, feeling a pull so hard he was dizzy.

"Oh!" Wren's breath hissed between her teeth, and she made a sudden, violent gesture. "Illusion hiding it."

Connor saw the air flicker a short distance away, and a low, crumbling stone house appeared among the scrubby bushes. He and Wren began to run.

Teressa paused in the shade of a tree and shook her damp hair back from her face.

The sun was getting warm, and some of the boys and girls in their silks and velvets were beginning to look overheated. Still, several played on. Mirlee shrieked with laughter, sounding just like a crow, her dress of lemon yellow brocade almost blinding in the sunlight.

Mirlee's uncertain temper was nothing new, but the prickly feelings of some of the others reflected the tension of the adults, Teressa thought. Garian and his friends had planned some kind of elaborate game, but apparently it had not been quite ready and moods were too uncertain for waiting.

She looked across the long lawn at the swarm of girls and boys helping themselves to food and drink from the tables set out under the oak trees. A few still continued with the games that Teressa had quickly introduced when, with nothing else to do, some of those with hot tempers had begun squabbling.

Garian and several others had wandered down to the stream, where they were trying to walk the length of a narrow tree that had fallen across the water. Nyl had already fallen in, of course, and he sat wrapped in a cloak, trying to look as if he didn't mind being roundly laughed at. Teressa wondered what Leila had thought as she watched in her scrystone, seeing these elegantly dressed young lords and ladies playing the games that Teressa and Wren had once played at the orphanage. *Not that I made the mistake of telling them where I learned the games,* Teressa thought wryly, fighting back a yawn. *Let them think I made them up.*

"Yawning, Princess?" A voice startled her.

Teressa turned, saw Hawk standing behind her. He wore a blue velvet tunic so dark his long black hair was nearly lost in its shadowy folds. His white shirt gleamed under the tunic's slashed sleeves. Otherwise he wore no ornaments. At his side was a plain-hilted saber heavier than the lightweight gold-chased ornamental rapiers now popular among the boys. As Teressa looked up at him, she wondered again what he saw in the likes of Garian and Perd.

"Are you bored?" Hawk asked, hands on hips.

She smiled politely. "Just a little tired."

"I think everyone's had plenty to eat," he said. "Let's start the real games." He raised his voice slightly: "Garian."

The thin figure standing on the log jerked his head up, and with a couple of bounds, he successfully made it to the shore. "Shall we divide into teams now?" he called, the sun making a blaze of his scarlet tunic.

Hawk nodded, and Garian's friends burst into cheers. At once everyone else demanded to know what was going on, and voices babbled in growing excitement as Garian shouted directions, waving people into two groups.

Teressa moved to join them.

"Wait," Hawk said.

Teressa looked up in surprise. "I don't know what team I'm on."

"You're on my team."

"It's already been decided?" Teressa asked in surprise.

Hawk nodded, grinning, his teeth very white in his tanned face. "It'll be fun. I promise."

Teressa turned her attention back to the group. It seemed to her that Garian had complete chaos on his hands, as boys and girls demanded loudly to be on one team or the other.

Finally they were all divided, and Garian pointed at one group, saying, "You wait here and count to two hundred. You others, go hide—but you can't go beyond the park boundaries."

The ones who were to stay behind sat down in a circle on the grass. Mirlee, who was one of them, stood up again and in a shrill voice started, "One . . . two . . . three . . ." The others joined in, their voices getting louder and louder. "Eight . . . nine . . . ten . . ."

"C'mon," Garian said to Teressa and Hawk, Marit and Perd running behind him. "Let's get going."

"What now?" Teressa asked.

"We're hiding," Garian said with his irritating smirk.

"I'd like to do that on my own," Teressa said.

"No, you've got to come with us," Marit said, smiling with surprising shyness. "It's part of the game."

"Here, someone got my note?" Garian said suddenly. "I don't have it."

"It's taken care of," Hawk said. "Let's get moving."

"Oh," Garian said, looking confused as he followed Hawk's lead.

They headed straight toward the thick growth of forest along the edge of the park.

Teressa walked along, repressing her feelings of annoyance. Garian was hosting this party, and she knew how important it was for the peace her parents were trying to win that she be a good guest. She said politely, "Why don't you explain the rules of this game to me?"

Garian frowned at the grass for a few steps. Finally he looked up, his expression now very confused. "Tell you the truth," he said, "I don't perfectly understand how it works. We're going to leave the ransom note for them to find, right?"

"That's the idea," Hawk said.

"Then what? I mean, what will they use in place of all that stuff I demanded?"

"Oh, they'll have to use their imaginations," Hawk said.

"What's going on?" Teressa asked the circle of boys around her.

"You're being kidnapped," Garian said, laughing.

"Watch out," Wren said, grabbing Connor's sleeve. "I think I better check for magic traps."

"Do you know how?" Connor asked.

"Well, not really," Wren admitted. "But I can tell if magic is on something, like the door. Let me feel first."

She put her hand to the rotting wooden door and felt nothing but rough splinters. She pushed against it, and when the door did not give, she pushed a little harder.

"Let me," Connor said. He put his shoulder to it and shoved.

The door creaked open, sending a flurry of dust motes swirling in the shaft of light that cut the thick darkness inside.

The room they entered had a little furniture, all well covered by spiderwebs. An old trunk lay in a corner; a few cracked dishes sat on a table. Otherwise the room was nearly empty.

"There's a room in the back," Connor said, pointing.

Wren stood where she was, letting her eyes adjust. She followed Connor.

That was when they heard a noise and stopped.

It came again, a rustle and a faint whine.

Connor slammed the door open, and there, sitting on

the floor, was a wire cage with a shape crammed in it. Wren could not make out what it was. Holding her nose against a dreadful smell, she advanced slowly.

Connor rushed right over and put his hand down to the cage. The creature in it whined, and Connor's head jerked up. "It's Tyron," he said, his voice cracking. "He's desperately sick."

"Let's get him out of there!" Wren cried.

Connor's hands were already tearing at the wire. He managed to pry open a tiny hole, but it was too small for Tyron to crawl out.

As Connor looked around for something to force the cage open, Wren exclaimed in a shaky voice, "I think it was closed around him by magic! Let me see the hinges."

She felt the joints and sensed the familiar magical buzz. Shutting her eyes, she remembered the lesson she'd learned about the bridge, how the magicians had strengthened ordinary materials to make it. She muttered, concentrating on reversing the spell. Faint blue light glowed at the corners of the cage—

"Ah!" Connor exclaimed, yanking the top of the cage apart.

Tyron struggled weakly to his feet, his hindquarters shaking. Wren's heart wrenched at the sight of his thin body and matted fur.

Tyron growled and whined, and Connor bent close to listen, then looked up to say, "It's that foreigner Hawk. Tyron says he's got them all fooled into thinking one of the adults is the sorcerer. But it's Hawk, and he's going to kidnap Teressa, *right now*."

Tyron whined again.

"We've got to change Tyron back," Wren said.

"We've got to rescue Teressa."

"That too, but the magic on him feels bad," Wren said. "I don't think we should wait."

"Can you do it?"

Wren shook her head slowly. "The magicians are all at

the ambassador's, and we dare not use the transport spell—Mistress Leila!"

Connor shook his head. "She's sound asleep in the palace, remember?"

Wren bit her lip. She couldn't worry about Mistress Leila. Something had to be done—now. "I can try . . . but I really don't know that kind of magic. Can't you do it, reversing what you did on your Basics Test?"

"And risk turning him into something worse?" Connor retorted bitterly. "I—wait." He paused, listening to Tyron's muffled yaps. "He says he can give you the words."

Wren wiped her sweaty palms. "All right."

Connor bent close to Tyron, and patiently, one at a time, he repeated the words of power needed.

Slowly Wren tried to shape the spell, but midway through she felt the magic leaching away, like fire through her fingers. She stopped, took a deep breath, and tried again. Her head buzzed as she felt power gathering in the little room—her eyes and ears blurred, and again she lost the spell. "It's too strong," she cried. "I can't do it."

Connor lifted his hands. "I *feel* it," he said. "The magic . . . I can almost shape it . . ." He frowned with concentration, then looked up suddenly. "Try again," he urged. "With me this time." He held out one hand.

Wren stepped near, and Connor closed his fingers around hers. Connor placed his other hand on Tyron's filthy fur, and Wren followed suit. They spoke the words in unison.

As she finished, she tried her best to see Tyron in place of the dog—and suddenly his outline began to blur.

A moment later she stared in amazement at Tyron's long, bare arms and his knobby spine as he lay on the floor, curled like an infant. "We did it, we *did* it!"

Connor knelt at Tyron's side. "He's unconscious," he said, his eyes dark with worry. "I don't remember you reacting like this last year."

Wren shook her head numbly. "He's been a dog too long," she said. "But he didn't give in."

181

"And it's nearly killed him," Connor murmured.

Wren stared down at Tyron's still, pale face. *Why didn't he become an animal?* she thought. She knew it must have taken a tremendous effort of will to hold off the final transformation. How had he done it? She remembered her own time as a dog. She had enjoyed it more than not, which—Halfrid told her later—had probably made her transition to her human self the easier.

I wonder if it has to do with imagination, she thought. *He doesn't have any and doesn't see any reason to have any. Maybe a certain amount of make-believe can be a protection.*

Her thoughts were splintered when Connor said, "I'll see if I can waken him. Why don't you check if there's some kind of clothing in that trunk out there?"

Wren nodded and ran out to the front room. Throwing the lid of the trunk back, she choked as a thick cloud of dust flew up into her face.

Inside she found a rotting blanket, a rough-woven cloak, and under that an old, patched, mildewed tunic.

"Found something," she called as loudly as she dared, catching up the clothing and tossing it through the door into the other room. "How is he?"

"He's waking up," came the welcome response.

Wren leaned against a wall in relief, then straightened again when she spotted something behind the trunk: a stout wooden staff. Clearing the spiderwebs from it with one hand, she grabbed the heavy length of wood. "Here's something else." She leaned the staff against the wall just inside the doorway.

Then she retreated to the front to make sure no one had discovered them. The air was suddenly sweet, and she sucked it in gratefully. *Well, that's another school rule I just broke,* she thought. *But we did it.*

A scrape behind made her turn her head. The boys appeared in the doorway, Tyron leaning heavily on Connor. Tyron's drawn, filthy face looked more foxlike than ever above the shabby trunk clothes. His mouth worked a moment, as if lips and teeth were unfamiliar. As though he had forgotten the use of his fingers, he clumsily grabbed up the staff Wren had found.

With a pang she remembered how hard it had been to move like a person and not a dog just after her own transformation. *And I'm sure I did not look as worn and sick as he does now.*

But Tyron's eyes were alert, and he managed his old grin, stretching dry, cracked lips. "Practicing ahead of your year, Wren?" he asked in a voice barely above a whisper.

She gave an unwilling laugh, then turned serious. "We've got to get to Teressa."

Connor yanked Garian's ransom note out of his tunic and thrust it in front of Tyron. "So Garian is Hawk's dupe, am I right?"

Tyron nodded, squinting at the note. "It's got to be a decoy. I think that paper is supposed to get the palace roused and searching for Garian."

"While Hawk makes off with Teressa." Wren looked at Connor. "You know, if I'd found that note, I wouldn't have questioned it."

Connor shook his head. "Garian's mean and he's a snob, but I don't believe he's a traitor."

"Right," Tyron said. "So the question is, where are they? Hawk doesn't think anyone will figure out his plot, and if I understand him—and I do, after being his prisoner this past few days—he'll enjoy spinning this out until the last moment. If we move fast, we might still have a chance to catch him by surprise."

"They're in the King's Park," Wren said. "Having a picnic."

"The park," Tyron said. "But that's huge. How do we find them in that?"

Connor smiled with relief. "Easy," he said. "Just let me ask some passing birds."

183

Chapter Eighteen

*T*eressa stopped and whirled around. "That's not funny," she said.

"Sure it is." Hawk gave a soft laugh, his dark eyes glittering.

"We're making all kinds of ridiculous demands," Garian said, gesturing airily. "They'll have to meet them, or else!"

"Or else what?" Teressa asked, no longer hiding her annoyance.

"Or else they'll lose," Garian said with a shrug. "What else? Although Mirlee will manage to make it into a feud somehow, you just watch. She's the worst loser ever born." He turned to Hawk. "We'll need a good hideout. You were supposed to see to that."

"I have," Hawk said as they reached a road, then crossed over it.

"But this is the border of the King's Park," Perd pointed out, looking around. "Didn't we set the boundaries at the border?"

"I never did," Hawk said as they passed among the trees in the woodland beyond the park. "And the best hideout is one that nobody can find. Why don't you three go back and make certain they're decoyed?"

"Plenty of time for that after we see where your hideaway is," Garian said.

"And you can sit in it alone," Teressa said suddenly. "You should have asked me first. I'm not going to be your hostage, and I'm staying in the park." She thrust past Perd and started back toward the road.

Hawk caught up in two swift strides, and he took her arm in a firm grip. "Too late," he said.

Teressa tried to pull away, and when he did not let go she jerked her arm. Hawk just held on, and she nearly lost her balance.

Garian's sharp face lifted. "Look, Hawk, you don't need to be rough."

"She's not cooperating," Hawk said, smiling.

Teressa winced at the steely grip on her arm. "Let me go," she demanded, looking around somewhat desperately. *Where's Aunt Leila? Is she watching in that magic stone of hers?* "Let me go. Now."

"All right," Hawk said.

He freed her suddenly, so suddenly she sat down hard on the grass.

"Time for your lot to decoy the others, Rhismordith," Hawk said.

Garian crossed his arms. "I thought it was *my* game," he said. "At least we can share the command. And I'll take charge of my cousin."

"I'm taking over now," Hawk said. "And she's my hostage."

Garian looked nonplussed, and Perd gaped. Marit reddened with anger.

Teressa glanced around, but her aunt was nowhere in sight. *I'm going to have to look out for myself,* she thought, and she got to her feet. She started walking in the opposite direction.

"Don't run off," Hawk said over his shoulder. "I need you right here."

"Go ahead and need," Teressa snapped, rubbing her arm. She increased her pace, her ears listening for steps in the grass.

They came, at a run. Teressa also started running, grabbing her skirts in bunches at either side.

"Wait—Hawk—this isn't funny," Garian called on a note that was partly warning and partly whine.

"Yes, it is," Hawk said. "And it's getting funnier all the time."

He caught up with Teressa right then, and he yanked her right off her feet. She hit the ground hard, rolling into a patch of mud. Her head crunched against a tree root, sending stars shooting across her vision.

Garian stopped. "What *did* you do with my note?" he demanded.

"It's sitting on Verne Rhisadel's desk." Hawk gave a cold laugh. "And he and his fools will be along soon, looking for your blood, so I suggest you cut along and hide."

Garian's face went crimson. "You *betrayed* me!"

"Right," Hawk said. "And you certainly made it easy."

"Stop him!" Garian yelled at his friends.

Teressa, looking up dizzily, saw Hawk almost lazily swing an arm and hit Perd across the face. The boy spun around and dropped, letting out a surprised howl. Then Hawk pulled his sword free.

Garian squawked something, yanking out his jeweled rapier.

Hawk laughed. "Funnier all the time," he repeated, striking Garian's rapier hard and causing the blade to bend. Garian staggered, raising his point in time to take another smashing blow. This time he lost his grip completely, the rapier falling to the grass.

Hawk lifted his blade and turned to Marit, who'd also pulled his sword. As Marit studied him doubtfully, Hawk ripped his blade under Marit's guard and stabbed the boy hard right in the shoulder. Garian got to his feet and rushed Hawk, yelling crazily. Stepping aside, Hawk used the hilt to club Garian hard across the back of his head. Garian fell down and lay still.

Despite her dizziness, Teressa got to her feet and once

again began to run. Behind her Perd gave a short exclamation, then she heard the crack of a fist—and then the pounding of fast footsteps.

"Now it's time for *us* to go," Hawk said to Teressa, closing his hand around her arm.

He started muttering softly. Alarm burned through her when she realized he was performing a magic spell. *It's Hawk. He's the sorcerer!*

Desperate to get free, she pretended to trip, and tore loose from his grasp. She landed on the grass, felt under her skirt for her boot—and her fingers closed around her little knife.

"Let's try that again," he said, breaking off his spell and reaching for her.

She whipped the blade out and slashed it across his hand.

Hawk gave a short exclamation and sprang back. Laughing in surprise, he studied her appraisingly for a moment. Then he pulled out his handkerchief and bound it around his bleeding hand.

"You're not as boring as I thought, cousin," he said, grinning. "You really ought to stay away from those court fools. They make you about as interesting as a wooden shoe."

Teressa got to her feet, her knife ready. "I know my cousins, and much as I dislike some of them, at least I can say that you're not one of them."

"We are distant cousins." Hawk bowed with mocking grace. "My full name is Hawk Rhiscarlan. I'm just about to take possession of my lands, now that your father has his cursed Scarlet Guard up here chasing phantoms. And you're coming with me as my bargaining counter."

"I'm not going anywhere," Teressa said between shut teeth. "And you're twice the fool if you think my father will believe that stuff about Garian and ransoms for more than half a day."

"But it will keep them busy—and it should also cause an almighty rift when our Rhismordith cousins have to live down the fact that Garian was my dupe."

"So you *were* the one causing all those problems. What a filthy thing to do!" Teressa exclaimed.

"It was just as filthy when my home was torched and my family killed off. All except my cousin Idres—wherever she is."

"Idres!" Teressa exclaimed.

Hawk's eyes narrowed. "You *know* her. How? Where?"

Teressa remembered the silent, black-haired woman who had helped with her rescue the year before. The magicians had been ambivalent about Idres, who was a very powerful magician but allied with no one, and her part in the adventure had been little spoken of. Now Teressa just shrugged. "I won't tell you," she said rudely, enjoying the flush of color that ridged Hawk's bony cheeks.

"I will find out," he said. "And I'll have fun doing it, too."

"You're wasting your breath with those stupid threats." She backed slowly, brandishing her knife. *Keep him talking until I figure out what to do.* "Anyway, it wasn't us who burned the Rhiscarlan Fortress, it was one of your own relatives—aided secretly by Andreus of Senna Lirwan."

Hawk shrugged. "Perhaps. But it was your father who was about to give away my lands to the Rhismordiths and their toadies." He stepped toward her, still keeping just out of reach. "Drop the blade," he warned. "I don't want to hurt you—"

"Well, I will be quite happy to hurt *you* again if you touch me," Teressa said, watching him warily.

Hawk held his empty hands a little way from his sides, one showing red through the white handkerchief. His dark eyes were steady on her as he took one step toward her, then another.

"The idea is to use you to keep your father at a distance while I consolidate my holdings," Hawk said. "And then you're free to do what you wish."

"You're free to leave right now," Teressa said. "But I'm not going with you."

188

"Don't you want to know the fate of your doggy magician friend?" Hawk taunted.

"Tyron?" Teressa exclaimed, almost stumbling.

Hawk smiled nastily at her reaction. "He's going to Andreus, who has a taste for revenge. See—I don't trust Andreus any more than I do your father and his collection of fools here in Cantirmoor."

"You plan to send Tyron to Andreus?" Teressa asked, backing up a step. *Keep him talking . . . keep him talking.* "That's disgusting. He never did anything to you, or to your family."

Hawk shrugged. "I have to keep Andreus busy while I strengthen my position," he said blandly, as though his plans were completely reasonable. "Also it serves as a kind of warning to him." He smiled again. "I wish I'd managed to catch the other two, but one person can only do so much—" He reached suddenly.

Teressa swept her blade in a fast arc, and Hawk faded back—then he lunged, bringing his hand down hard across her wrist.

Giving a sharp cry, she dropped the knife.

"Now we'll—"

"Now you'll let her go," a new voice said.

Hawk whirled around, staring in surprise at the three figures who came slowly toward them, the short and tall outside ones supporting the fox-faced one in the middle.

"Wren!" Teressa cried in relief. "Connor—*Tyron!*"

Wren saw Hawk point at Teressa, and magic gleamed around her for a moment. Teressa sank slowly onto the grass.

"He's put a weight spell on her," Tyron muttered, trying to straighten up. "It can't last. Keep him busy so he can't transport with her."

Tyron looked awfully pale, but his hands were steady, glowing with a greenish light that suddenly shot across the grassy sward toward Hawk.

"No!" Hawk said, raising his hand and uttering a short phrase. The greenish light glittered, then disappeared. "My other three targets. How convenient." He started weaving a spell.

Wren could feel power building, like a cold wind drawing lightning-charged air toward Hawk. Terrified, she knew she couldn't counter it. Beside her, Tyron blinked away the backwash from his last spell. He wasn't strong enough to fight magic with magic.

But before Hawk could finish his spell, Connor jerked the staff from Tyron's weak fingers and ran straight at Hawk.

The dark-haired magician broke off his spell and whipped out his sword, grinning as the weapons met with a loud crack.

Wren caught desperately at Tyron, who swayed unsteadily.

"Can't—breathe," Tyron whispered, blinking hard. He made a blind swipe in the air with one hand, fingers curled like a paw.

Wren turned her eyes from him to the fight before her. Connor was good with the staff, but Hawk seemed equally adept with his sword. Still, Connor whistled loudly as he tried to edge Hawk away from Teressa, who still lay frozen on the grass.

What can I do? Wren thought, trying to ignore Connor's whistles. *Oh!* she thought suddenly. *That's what Connor's doing—he's making it hard to concentrate.*

"So you are the fungus-faced slimecrawler who ruined my Basics Test?" Wren yelled at Hawk, adding her own confusion.

Hawk laughed, throwing her a fast glance, then he swung the sword at Connor in a deadly arc. "You're good, prentice," he called to her. "Your magic shows promise and you and Lackland gave my hirelings a fine run. Too bad I was too busy here to come after you myself. We would have seen some sport. But I think Andreus will enjoy you when he does catch up with you."

"He'd better get running," Wren said. "Because it's going to take three lifetimes to find us. As for you—Halfrid will be here in a moment. We summoned him." She held up her scrystone. It winked in the sunlight.

Once again Hawk sent her a fast glance, his eyes narrowed. "He can't. I ruined his transport setup."

"And he fixed it, but he didn't let on," Wren crowed.

Next to her, Tyron took in a deep, shuddering breath and started muttering. He clapped his hands suddenly, and weak light streamed out.

Hawk whirled his sword toward Connor, who raised his staff. Steel bit into wood, sending up a thin wisp of smoke. Then Hawk threw one hand up and gasped out a word. Tyron's glow turned and dove into the ground.

"You'll have to do better—than that," he called, but he was panting as Connor grimly pressed to the attack. Hawk started muttering in a low voice, his eyes narrowed to thin points of light as he concentrated on Connor.

Watching him, Tyron started yet another spell, but Hawk finished his first. Tyron threw up a hand and croaked out a single word to deflect it. Wren felt a weird scraping along her bones, and a low hum filled the air, then faded.

"Here comes Halfrid, moldmouth!" Wren called, but this time Hawk ignored her.

What can I do? What can I do? Wren yanked off her sash with one hand, bent to pick up a good stone. Slinging it at Hawk, she watched in dismay when he saw it, broke off his spell, and ducked, then whirled to cut another chunk from Connor's staff.

Connor, meanwhile, was still whistling.

Hawk began yet another spell. But before he got far, the trees began to rustle. A hundred birds exploded out from the leaves, cawing and cheeping and screeching, just as a final sword's blow shattered the wood in Connor's hands.

Connor backed away and pointed, and winged shapes descended upon Hawk in a spiraling storm. Hawk jerked his head up, striking out at the closest birds with his fist. For the first time, Teressa stirred weakly on the ground.

Wren did not wait a moment longer. Stepping away from Tyron, she ran across the grass and pulled Teressa to her feet.

"Stop—" Hawk said, starting toward them.

Wren kicked out at his legs. "Stop yourself, rotnose—"

A huge bird shrieked right near Hawk's head, forcing him to duck from the extended claws.

While he was busy with the birds, the girls moved away from him.

"Good work, Wren," Connor said when the two girls reached him.

For a moment they stood thus, the four ranged together before Hawk. "Spell," Tyron whispered. "Help me . . . keep him busy . . ."

"Oh—here they are!"

They all turned to see Garian coming at a clumsy run, one hand clenching his sword and the other pressed against the side of his head. Some distance behind him stumbled Marit, clutching his shoulder, and Perd, with a swelling jaw.

"Just a moment longer," Tyron murmured, his eyes closed. His shaking hands made a gesture as he intoned a long phrase. Light started to glow in front of him, rapidly gaining power.

Hawk's eyes narrowed; he glanced from Tyron to Garian and then back at the four. Then he grinned. "The comedy is about to become a farce," he called. "I'll leave you to it." He saluted them with his sword, muttering softly.

Then he vanished, the grass where he'd been standing waving wildly in a ruffle of wind. The birds shrieked and whistled in alarm, and departed with a great beating of wings.

Garian lurched to a stop and stood gaping. "Lackland?" he said weakly. "How'd you get here?"

Connor's jaw tightened, but he said nothing.

Wren felt Teressa stir in her grasp and step forward. Despite the mud and grass stains that had ruined her gown and covered her face and arms, Teressa looked very much like a princess right now. An *angry* princess.

"Shut up, Garian," she said, not in her usual soft, careful voice, but loud and angry and shrill. "Just *shut up*. If I ever hear you say that again, I'll tell everyone just what a dupe you've been. And I'll call you Lack*wit*."

Connor blinked at Teressa, his face turning a fiery red. Teressa smiled tentatively at him, then she too blushed.

Silently, Connor walked over to Garian and handed him a crumpled paper.

"What's—" Garian looked down at it and gulped.

"We'll say nothing if you don't," Connor said. Then he turned to his friends. "Let's go."

Wren chortled, holding tightly to Teressa's hand. "I don't know about you, but I'm hungry, and Tyron, you better get a bath before our noses fall off. Whew, you stink!"

Epilogue

*W*ren stretched luxuriously, contemplating her new sandals. "Ahhh," she sighed happily.

Teressa looked over her shoulder. She was seated on a rock above a little waterfall in the King's Park. Her feet were bare, splashing in the water. "What was that for, Wren?"

Wren lay back and crossed her arms behind her head, staring up through the interlacing tree branches at the blue sky overhead. "I'm pleased how things came out."

Teressa wrinkled her nose. "I'm glad one person is. Papa has been in a bear of a temper over how Hawk fooled us all."

"Mistress Leila was pretty sour about drinking the sleep-potion that Hawk's spy slipped her," Wren said.

"Papa's also mad about how easily Hawk sneaked his people into the old Rhiscarlan Fortress. He's entrenched there now. Only a war can get him out, and Papa's not willing to go to that extreme unless Hawk starts one first."

"What I won't forgive is what Hawk did to Tyron."

Teressa looked serious. "Aunt Leila said it will take him some time to recover, but the fact that he made the transformation back to human at all still has them amazed."

Wren nodded. "Halfrid told me—where Tyron couldn't hear and be embarrassed—that he will be a very great magician some day." She was silent a moment. "But I'd like to

195

turn Hawk into something nasty. How could one person cause so much damage?"

A voice spoke behind them. "He obviously had it planned for years."

Tyron and Connor appeared, pushing their way through overhanging branches. They emerged into the sunlight, and Connor set a heavy basket down. Tyron dropped onto the grass near Wren, his thin, bony face tired.

"He has plenty of money, which explains how he had so many spies running about, spreading rumors and causing fights," Connor continued.

"And he learned a lot growing up, watching the court battles in Fil Gaen," Tyron added, stretching out on the grass. "Apparently their squabbles are ten times worse than ours."

"What I can't figure out," Wren said, "is why he was after Connor and me, since we hadn't done anything to him."

"I think he wanted to grab us to show Andreus he could do it," Connor said, starting to set wrapped packets of food out on a blanket. "Partly to show off, partly as a challenge."

Tyron twirled a blade of grass between his fingers. "Halfrid hasn't been able to find out who trained Hawk in magic, though."

"Andreus?" Wren asked.

Tyron shook his head. "No. But they seem to be allies—of a sort."

"Food's ready," Connor said.

Wren scooted over, and Teressa swung gracefully to her feet, brushing her skirts out. Wren saw Connor watching, but as soon as Teressa looked up at them to smile, Connor went back to passing cups around.

Grabbing up a peach, Wren bit into it. *They don't seem to be so uncomfortable with each other anymore, but they aren't exactly talking like old friends.* She frowned, noticing Tyron's eyes on her. He was grinning in a funny way.

"What is it?" she asked. "If you're going to point out I've just slopped peach juice down my front, I already know it."

Tyron shook his head lazily. "Not me," he said, holding up his palm. "After the way I looked when I got out of Hawk's cage, I don't think I'll ever have anything to say about anybody's appearance again. I still get tired at the oddest moments. But this I do swear: I will never shape-change again."

"Here. Eat something." Teressa handed him a breadroll stuffed with sausage. "Aunt Leila's instructions."

"Why'd it take you two so long to get here, anyway?" Wren asked.

"Garian," Tyron said, then took a huge bite from his bread.

"He hasn't started his nastiness again?" Wren asked, aghast.

"Worse," Connor said. "He came to apologize."

"A sorry Garian is even less appetizing than a sniffy Garian," Tyron added. "It was pretty grim."

"I think he knows very well that if your roles had been reversed, he would have wasted no time in running to the ambassador's and raising the biggest dust possible," Teressa said, her eyes dark and intense. A little color suddenly entered her cheeks. "It was a handsome thing to do, Connor, giving that stupid ransom note back to him and promising silence. Even Perd and Marit were impressed."

"I felt sorry for him," Connor said. "He'd lost more than a scuffle with a villain, and I think he knew it."

Silence fell, everyone busy with their own thoughts. When Wren glanced up, she saw that Tyron had fallen asleep, a half-eaten sandwich still in his hand. Teressa had pulled a book from her pocket, and Connor was walking slowly downstream.

Wren scrambled to her feet and followed.

"Well?" she said. "Did you give the play to the Master Playwright?"

Connor winced. "I did, under a false name. And I got an honest response: He thought it was dreadful. And worse, when I reread it last night, I saw that he was right."

"But you put all that real experience in it," Wren protested. "How could—"

"It was those additions that made it terrible," Connor explained. "Master Salek said, 'This is a play about how bad the roads are, not about the heroism of two wizards.' " Connor stared down at the rushing water. "I don't think I'm meant to be a playwright," he said. "The thought of writing it over and over until it suits someone else destroys the fun."

"So what now?" Wren asked. "Back to the fish-folk?"

"Perhaps," Connor said, looking up at the sky. "But not yet. I'm afraid that once I make my visit, I will still be facing the same decision about what to do with my life."

Wren opened her mouth to say something, but they both heard voices uptrail and turned their heads. "Tyron's awake again," Wren said.

They walked back to the picnic site. Book in lap, Teressa was laughing, and Tyron was finishing his sandwich.

"So, Wren," Tyron said, "are you glad you made your quest?"

"Of course!" Wren exclaimed as she sat down in her place. "I love my Aunt Niss, and I hope someday to find my father."

"So what's your next plan?" Tyron asked. "Just give me plenty of warning."

"Well, the inn is nice, and I'll love to visit, but it isn't home," Wren said. "I think I'll have to travel a little farther, maybe after I pass to journeymage—" She stopped, frowning. "What do you mean, warning?"

Tyron lifted a hand. "Of your next adventure, what else?"

"Huh?"

Tyron sat up. "Every time you make a trip, something happens. If you ever decide to go around the world, we'll somehow all get messed in with five terrible sorcerers, a couple of sea monsters"—he paused as Teressa and Connor laughed—"not to mention a haunted castle, a map with a mysterious curse on it, and—"

198

Wren sighed. "Oh, I just *wish* that would happen."

"No, no, I take it back," Tyron said, collapsing back into the grass. "Forget it! Peace and quiet, that's what we need. At least twenty years of it. Forty!"

"I wonder if our adventures *are* all over," Wren said wistfully. "It would be, well, *greedy* to wish for more." But she remembered the old sorcerers the Sendimerys Twins saying last year after she and Tyron and Connor had returned from rescuing Teressa, *Train these young people well.* "Train us for what?" she wondered.

Then she thought about Andreus of Senna Lirwan, plotting away in his stronghold, and Hawk, now busy in the south of Meldrith.

No, Wren thought, *our adventures are not over. Not over at all.*

She looked up at the sky through the trees, and smiled.

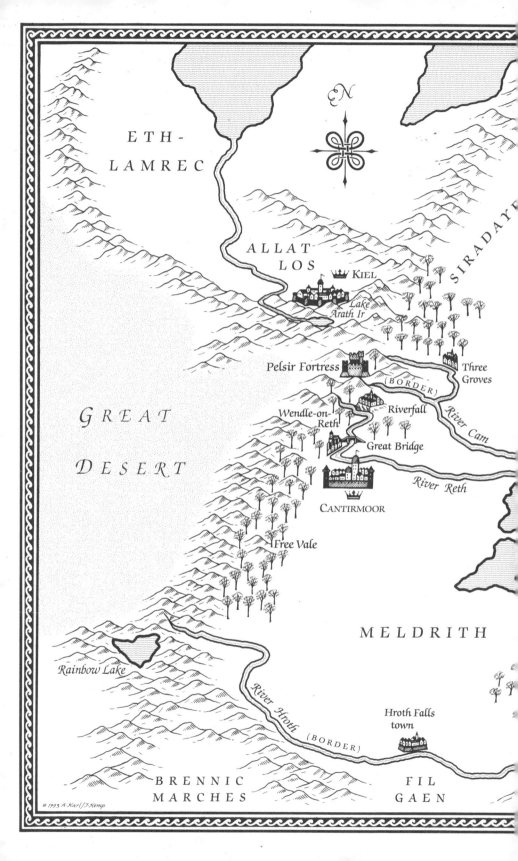